PRAISE
for yellow dog

An exhilarating ride through the icy wilderness of
Northern Saskatchewan, Miriam Körner's *Yellow Dog*
is a beautiful exploration of a traditional way of life
that is quickly becoming extinct.

—National Reading Campaign

With a true natural born storyteller's skill,
novelist Miriam Körner is able to deftly craft
an impressively engaging and entertaining read
that will make *Yellow Dog* an enduringly popular
addition to personal reading lists and community library
General Fiction collections.

—Midwest Book Review

Heartwarming and optimistic.

—Kirkus

This very Canadian coming of age novel
set on a reserve in northern Saskatchewan
could become a classic …
—Resource Links

Körner, a Saskatchewan resident and sled dog owner,
vividly portrays life in the Canadian north, including a
shocking scene with a stray dog, and seeds the novel
with authentic dog team culture and history.
VERDICT Hand this touching coming-of-age
adventure to fans of Gary Paulsen's *Hatchet*.
—School Library Journal

I found reading *Yellow Dog* both interesting and nostalgic.
A wonderful tale of maturing, understanding and forgiveness
by renewing a way of life that has all but disappeared …
—Keith Olsen, author of *Within the Stillness: One Family's Winter
on a Northern Trapline*

A Canadian Children's Book Center Best Book Selection

Nominated for the MYRCA

A Saskatchewan Book Award Finalist

YELLOW DOG

A COMING-OF-AGE NOVEL

MIRIAM KÖRNER

Red Deer Press

Published in Canada by Red Deer Press,
195 Allstate Parkway, Markham, ON L3R 4T8

Published in the United States by Red Deer Press,
311 Washington Street, Brighton, Massachusetts 02135

www.reddeerpress.com   rdp@reddeerpress.com

10 9 8 7 6 5 4 3

Red Deer Press acknowledges with thanks the Canada Council for the Arts,
and the Ontario Arts Council for their support of our publishing program.

We acknowledge the financial support of the Government of Canada.

Library and Archives Canada Cataloguing in Publication
Körner, Miriam, 1975-, author
Yellow dog / Miriam Körner.

ISBN 978-0-88995-546-2 (paperback)
I. Title.
PS8621.O785Y45 2016   jC813'.6   C2016-904366-5

Publisher Cataloging-in-Publication Data (U.S.)
Names: Körner, Miriam, author.
Title: Yellow Dog / Miriam Körner.
Description: Markham, Ontario : Red Deer Press, 2016. | Summary: "In this
coming of age adventure story, a thirteen year old boy learns to train sled dogs in
Northern Saskatchewan. Along with his team of dogs he learns important
lessons in patience, focus and self-discipline" – Provided by publisher.
Identifiers: ISBN 978-0-88995-546-2 (paperback)
Subjects: LCSH: Coming of age -- Fiction. | Sled dogs – Canada – Fiction. |
Adventure stories, Canadian. | BISAC: YOUNG ADULT FICTION / Coming of Age.
Classification: LCC PZ7.1K676Ye | DDC 813.6 – dc23

Edited for the Press by Peter Carver
Text and cover design by Tanya Montini
Front cover images courtesy of the author
Printed in Canada

To Mooshum—
and all your good memories of a life
that was anything but easy

CHAPTER 1

"Hey, Jeremy! Dare yah to pull *that* dog's tail."

Justin's smug smile says it all. He doesn't think I'm gonna do it. To be honest, I'd rather not. It's not that I'm scared of that scruffy yellow dog. Although it doesn't exactly help that a dog bit Justin's brother just a couple days ago. It didn't even look all that vicious compared to this dog here. If it wasn't for the yellow color of his fur, I'd say he almost looks like a wolf.

"Come on, Jeremy, I don't have all day. If you're too chicken, just say so." Justin walks a few steps down the dusty gravel road like he has lost all interest. His back is turned to me, but I can still feel his eyes digging into me, sharp as a knife.

I don't really understand what Justin's problem is with dogs. I never thought much of it, when it was just throwing rocks. We all did that. But something is different now, and I don't know if Justin just got meaner or I just don't enjoy it so much anymore. I mean, it's easy to just throw a rock and watch the dog snap at the air, not knowing what attacked him, but if you hit a dog or pull its tail and the dog actually knows it's you ...

I quickly put the thought aside and squeeze through the opening in the fence. The yellow dog is sleeping by the front step—or what's left of it. Man, this house is in bad shape. It's not like any of the houses in Poplar Point would ever make the front cover on one of those "Happy Living" magazines, or whatever they're called. I don't even know why my mom reads them. But that's not the point. The point is that this house looks old, real old. The windows are either boarded up or covered in plastic. It doesn't have vinyl siding like the other houses. It's made of real logs. They are all silver gray. Like the driftwood by the beach.

I try to sneak up on the dog, but I'm still ten feet away when he opens his eyes. He gets up very slowly. His dark eyes look right through me, like he's trying to figure out if I'm the predator or the prey. I quickly pick up a couple rocks—just in case. And then the strangest thing happens. The dog wags his tail. Just ever so slightly. Why?

My muscles tense. I'm ready to bolt. But the dog rolls over like a puppy that wants a belly rub. I crouch down and reach for his tail. This is a lot easier than I thought. All I have to do now is pull and run. Only I can't.

I rest my hand on the dog's belly and glance over my shoulder. Justin is watching me from the fence.

"Sorry, pal," I whisper and yank his tail. The yellow dog yips as if he'd just stepped into a wasps' nest. He scrambles to his feet and turns in tight circles, snapping at his back end. His tail hangs between his legs—like a lifeless rag. I bite my lip. I don't think I pulled that hard.

I hear laughter from the fence but it sounds far away,

like when you're just waking up from a bad dream. Only this isn't a dream.

"I didn't think you had it in you, man!" Justin slaps me on the back.

I don't remember how I got to the other side of the fence. Justin smiles at me like I proved myself worthy of his friendship. But today, this doesn't make me proud.

"Are you crying?!" It sounds like Justin is whipping one word out after the other. "I. Can't. Believe. It."

"It's just dust, you idiot!" I push Justin and walk away. The yellow dog's cry is stinging in my ears.

CHAPTER 2

It snowed last night. Poplar Point is kind of pretty when it's all covered in white. It looks clean and fresh, like something out of a fairy tale. The snow crunches under my feet; the air is crisp and ...

"Ouch!" A snowball hits me on the back of my head.

"Hey, Jeremy! Where are you going?"

Justin. I've been avoiding him in school. Just didn't feel like talking to him.

"Home," I say and continue down the road.

"Wanna play video games at my house tonight?"

"Sure," I say, even though I've got no intention of going there. Not today.

"See you later, then," Justin says, but I don't reply.

When I reach our house, I look back. No sign of Justin on the road. So I walk past our house to the old cabin at the edge of town.

The yellow dog is sleeping in a tipped-over barrel on dusty blankets. There's smoke coming out the chimney. I wonder who lives there. It's kind of strange that I never noticed this place until I was here with Justin the other day. I mean, the cabin is at the end of the road and kind of tucked away in the bush, but still—Poplar Point isn't all that big.

I don't feel comfortable walking into someone else's yard, but I really want to see the yellow dog. I still feel bad about what I did and I want the feeling to go away. I open the gate as quietly as I can. The dog crawls deeper into the barrel and bares his teeth. I don't expect him to be all happy to see me, and yet, it makes my stomach feel all tight that he's so ... mad? Or scared? I really didn't mean to hurt him. I wish he would know that.

"Come here, Yellow Dog. It's okay," I say as I step closer.

The growling gets louder. I back up. What if he gets even with me now? He's got an impressive set of teeth. No question they can do some real damage.

"I'm sorry, okay? I won't do it again. No matter what." It's not like he can understand me, but talking to him makes me feel better. Like I am making a promise to myself that it's not going to happen again.

I dig in my school bag for my sandwich and slowly hold it out to Yellow Dog. He stops growling but he doesn't take it. I drop the sandwich into his barrel house. He doesn't touch it. I feel bad, because it's Justin's half that's lying in the dirt.

★

Justin always teases me about being thirteen and still getting my lunch packed by my mom. But he never says no when I offer him half. I don't know if his mom ever made him sandwiches. Not since we've been friends, and that's ages ago.

"What's for lunch?" Justin had asked at recess.

I told him I forgot it at home. I was going to save the whole sandwich for the dog, but then I got hungry and I secretly ate half of it in the boys washroom.

"I'm so hungry I could eat a whole moose," Justin joked when I came out. I couldn't look Justin in the eye so I looked at my feet. There was a ketchup drip on my boot from my moose meat sandwich.

★

I sigh.

"I saved it for you," I tell the dog and push the sandwich further into the barrel.

Yellow Dog presses harder against the back wall. He breathes fast. Too fast. His whole body is shaking. I back away and he relaxes a bit.

"Don't be scared." I take another step back.

Yellow Dog gently grabs the sandwich and picks out the meat. Most of the scrawny dogs I know would have eaten meat, bread,

AND my hand. Whoever is living in that cabin must look after him. Come to think of it, I never see him roam, either, even though he's not tied up. There's a whole gang of them chasing after the girl dogs and fighting over scraps. Yellow Dog isn't one of them.

I sit in front of his barrel, talking softly. Finally, he sticks his head out of the barrel and sniffs my hand. When I try to pet him, he ducks away and growls. Still, I'm happy. The sandwich was a good investment after all.

"See you later," I say and surprise myself. I had no intention of coming back but, as soon as I say it, I know I will.

★

Mom's home when I get back. I must have spent more time with Yellow Dog than I thought.

"How was school, Jeremy? Justin was here a minute ago. Wanted to know where you were."

Mom looks at me like it was *her* question and not Justin's.

I don't know what to say. I don't want to tell her about

the trouble with Justin, because I don't even know if we have trouble. And I don't want to tell her about Yellow Dog, either. What would I say? I was feeding the sandwich you made me to some scruffy dog that might never be able to wag his tail again? Somehow I sense that wouldn't fly without some further discussion. But I don't want to lie to her, either.

"Actually," I begin—and then it comes to me so quick that it nearly sounds like the truth—"I was just over at Justin's, looking for him."

"So you should have met him on the road."

Geez. Once you start with a lie, you have to invent more lies to keep the first one going. Or think it through better. Or simply don't lie.

"I did meet him. Just came in to grab a sandwich. Do we have some more leftover meat? The sandwich you made me this morning was really awesome."

Mom opens the fridge and passes me moose meat and margarine. I quickly slab a sandwich together.

"Don't eat too much before supper—I made stew and bannock."

Right. Friday. Mom gets off work early on Fridays, and usually she cooks up a storm of stews and soups and stuff to last for the whole week. If we run out before the week is over, it's KD or KFC.

"Save me some if I'm late." I rush out the door, sandwich in hand.

"Don't be too late, okay?"

It's more a question than an order. Mom's always been good about letting me do my thing. Maybe it's because I don't have a dad. He died in an accident just before I turned three. I don't remember him, and Mom never talks about him.

Or maybe it's because she just trusts me. I feel a twinge in my stomach. I shouldn't have lied. It's like I jumped out of the frying pan and into the fire. I just wanted to … I don't know. Not have Mom bug me with questions, I guess. Last thing I wanted, though, was to see Justin.

★

Justin is sitting on the front steps of his house, flinging rocks at the ravens with his slingshot. The dump truck must be broken. Garbage is spilling out of the bins everywhere. And even though it's cold, there's a rank smell in the air. A raven's paradise.

There are always different relatives staying at Justin's house, and I don't even know if the diapers the ravens are picking at belong to his youngest brother or cousin or nephew. It's kind of strange to think of Justin as an uncle. He doesn't look like fourteen when he's sitting there so slumped down and aiming listlessly at the ravens. He looks a lot younger. He looks like …

I suddenly think of Yellow Dog after I pulled his tail. He looked so betrayed, so hurt, so afraid. I want to turn around and run away before Justin sees me. But I can't go on avoiding him forever.

"How many did you get?" I ask him, just to break the ice.

Justin jumps when he sees me. His shoulders straighten; his stare turns hard like his voice.

"Get what?" he asks as he rubs his cheek.

"Ravens." I nod toward the two ravens that are fighting over a soggy french fry. "How many did you hit?"

"Oh, I didn't count." Justin stuffs his slingshot into his pocket.

"Let's go in and play some games."

"Nah, I'd rather not go in."

I hear adults yelling at each other through the closed door and nod. In situations like this, I'm almost glad that I only have one parent.

"Let's go," Justin says and quickly walks away.

When we walk by the east side of the house, I notice Justin's bedroom window is broken.

"What happened to the …"

"Nothing," Justin says before I can finish my question.

I don't know what to say, so I pull out the sandwich that I made before I left.

"Here."

Justin shakes his head. "No, thanks."

"I looked for a moose, but all I found is this old sandwich

I forgot this morning at home." I break it in half and, this time, Justin takes the other half.

"Even if you did see a moose, that wouldn't help you," he manages to grin with his mouth full. "You're such a lousy hunter."

"Who needs to hunt, anyways? We got KFC," I joke back, and it's almost like before the whole incident with the dog. Almost.

★

We walk to the schoolyard simply because we can't think of anywhere else to go. In summertime, that's where we meet. Mostly we just hang out or practice some tricks on our skateboards and bikes. In winter, nothing much happens here.

The only other living beings are two dogs in the process of producing puppies. First time I ever saw it, I thought someone had tied two dog tails together. I still remember how Justin gave me a lesson in sex education. First about the dogs, then about the humans. I think he was more knowledgeable about the dog business. I feel myself blushing just thinking of it. Good thing it's just about dark.

Suddenly, an ear-piercing yelp cuts through the silence. One of the dogs growls and bites into the air, dragging the other dog along. That one screams like someone is trying to kill it. It must be the girl dog. She snaps at her own rear end, but she can't pull away until the mating is over. I want to run to her and calm her down, but then I realize that Justin is firing rocks at the dogs.

"STOP! STOP! STOP!" I barely recognize my own voice. It's high-pitched and out of control. "You're hurting her! She can't get away!"

Justin laughs and reloads his slingshot.

"Here's another one for you, you filthy hounds. Don't need any more of you running around and biting little kids." Justin's voice is hard and cold and sounds a lot older. He walks over to the bushes and breaks off a willow.

"Leave them alone!" I start beating Justin's back with my fists. Not because I want to fight. It's just that I don't know what else to do. Justin turns around and pins me to the ground.

I don't fight back. When Justin gets off, the dogs are gone.

We walk off the playground in opposite directions.

★

I try not to think about Justin. But the harder I try, the more I think about him. It's the weekend, and there hasn't been a weekend that I didn't hang out with Justin. Sometimes Justin drags his little brother along. Isaac's only five and can be a real nuisance, but I know Justin is pretty proud of him. He doesn't let anybody else tease Isaac. Only Justin is allowed to do that.

Justin taught me how to swim, and I caught my first fish out on the lake with him and his dad. It doesn't sound like a big deal now but, back then, it was. Somehow I miss him, even though it was only yesterday that we fought, and even though I'm really, really mad at him. I still don't understand what happened last night. It's like he snapped and wasn't himself anymore.

I can kind of understand the business of shooting ravens with a slingshot. We all did that at some time. The first time I was a good enough shot to hit something, I killed a squirrel. I still remember its tiny black eyes. So pretty and yet so dead. Justin called me a princess, because I buried it under a tree and put a little wooden cross on it. A day later, I saw a dog running around with it, the squirrel's fur caked with dirt and blood. Maybe it was just a coincidence and it was some other squirrel, but I never tried to hit one again after that.

Justin is different, though. I mean, you don't have to like dogs. And there are a lot of mean dogs out there. But last night, there was something about Justin that scared me. I never thought he could really hurt someone. After last night, I'm not so sure anymore. It was like he didn't even see it was a dog. It could have been anything—or anyone. Strange thing is that I felt sorry for him. He didn't look like he had fun doing what he did. It just seemed like something he *needed* to do. I don't know how to explain it.

But then I have to think about the girl dog and the way she snapped blindly at her own rear end, because of a pain inside she couldn't stop. To hell with Justin.

CHAPTER 3

Yellow Dog isn't in his barrel. I feel a bit stupid, standing there with a sausage in my hand. What if the owner sees me? I glance over to the old house. There's a chopping block with a rusty axe and some split logs on top of the fresh snow. But nobody there.

I'm just about to turn around when I feel something cold and wet brushing against my hand. I stand still and let the dog sniff me. Very carefully, I open my hand and Yellow Dog takes the sausage. He walks out of my reach and gobbles it down.

I gasp for air. I hadn't even noticed I was holding my breath. I watch him eat and he watches me.

MIRIAM KÖRNER

"Hey, buddy," I say and kneel down in the snow.

Yellow Dog walks toward me. His butt is kind of wiggling, but his tail is still lifeless. I stretch my hand out to him. He cowers down and backs up.

"It's okay," I tell him. "Everything will be all right." I'm not sure why I'm telling him this. Nothing about this whole thing with Justin and Yellow Dog's tail is all right, but when I say it, it kind of feels right—at least for the moment.

Yellow Dog sniffs my hand and then he licks it. His tongue feels rough and it tickles my skin, but in a good way.

"Friends?" I ask and pet him under the chin. His fur feels coarse and greasy. But I don't care. For the first time in days, I feel good.

"He is a special dog, that one."

I jump. I didn't hear anybody coming, but there's an old man sitting on the front step, watching me. Yellow Dog wiggles his way over to the old man when he hears his voice, and the old man strokes him with stiff hands.

I can't help noticing that he's extra gentle when he comes to the dog's back end, where his lifeless tail is hanging. Does he know what I did? I feel like running as fast and far as I can, but I know if I run now, I'll never come back.

"He's really nice, sir," I say, and then I feel stupid because I couldn't think of anything better to say.

I don't know why the "sir" came out. Justin's cousin says it when he's pumping gas at Andy's after school. "Thank you, sir." "Have a good evening, ma'am." I always think it sounds kind of nice, like from an old movie or something. At school, the Elders want us to call them *moshōm* or *kohkom*, but I always had a hard time with calling someone grandfather or grandmother. Maybe because I never had my own grandparents. We call our teachers Mr. Ratt or Mrs. Charles or whatever their names are. But I don't know the old man's name and I don't know how to ask him, so I point to the dog by the old man's feet.

"What's his name?"

"Acimosis."

The dog's ears perk up when he hears his name and his back end wiggles.

"Acimosis?" I ask. I don't speak Cree, just the odd bits and pieces you learn at Cree culture class or from someone's *kohkom*, but I'm pretty sure that *acimosis* means puppy. Only Yellow Dog isn't exactly a puppy anymore. In fact, the hair around his muzzle is just as gray as the old man's.

I want to ask the old man if it's okay if I come and visit Acimosis, but I don't want to sound rude or embarrass myself anymore. I think about leaving when Yellow Dog—I mean Acimosis—rubs against my legs. I bury my hands in his long fur.

"Acimosis, so that's your name, then? And what makes you so special?"

I blush. Somehow it's easier to talk to the dog than to the old man, but then I realize how stupid that must sound. I look up, but the old man doesn't really seem to notice me. It's like he's looking at something behind me, something only he can see.

"He looks just like his father, doesn't he?" And then he nods toward me—or is it the dog? I'm not sure which.

"He would have made a fine *otapewatim*."

I don't know what that means, and I'm still not sure if he's talking to the dog or me, but I get that weird feeling that he somehow knows me or knows something about me. I'm getting creeped out.

"I have to go," I tell the old man.

The old man nods. "All these years, but you remember him, don't you?"

Who is he talking to? Me? The dog? Or someone else?

★

Mom is in the kitchen when I come home.

"Who lives in the old house on the hill, Mom?"

Mom empties a package of pasta into the cook pot. "Which one?"

"The really old log cabin at the end of the road."

MIRIAM KÖRNER

"Why do you want to know?"

My mother's voice suddenly sounds sharp. Not at all like her usual friendly voice. I don't know what to say.

"Jeremy! I'm asking you a question."

I suddenly feel like I've done something wrong, only I don't know what.

"Just wondering," I say.

Mom nods toward the dining room table. "Dinner is ready. Grab the plates. And don't ever go to that place."

After supper, I check out the online Cree dictionary, but I can't find *otapewatim*. Maybe I got the spelling wrong, but who knows how to spell Cree, anyway? Even our Cree language teacher doesn't know how to spell things. His excuse is that it's an oral language that was never meant to be written down. I wish English was an oral language. I could do without those spelling tests.

But that's not the point. The point is: it's kind of sad that I couldn't understand what the old man said, even though we live in the same community. I think there are only two kids in my class who speak Cree fluently, even though way more than half live on the rez. I guess I could ask one of the Elders what *otapewatim* means. Or I could just ask the old man. That would be the easiest. But what if he's crazy or dangerous, or both?

I think about asking Justin to come with me. He'd crack some joke and we'd laugh and there would be no reason to be creeped out. But then I realize how impossible the whole situation is. How would I tell Justin that I'm suddenly friends with that dog? I know I couldn't pretend I wasn't. And I could never do again what I did to him. Ever.

And how would I explain to Justin that I want to talk to an old man I don't even know? I can't even explain that to myself.

And all that is just the easy part. How can I even talk to Justin after our fight on Friday night?

CHAPTER 4

It's snowing so hard that I can't see from one power pole to the next. But I don't mind. Nobody will see me go to the end of the road.

Acimosis is not there, but there are dog tracks leading to the back of the house. I follow his paw prints around the old building. The first thing I see are rusty traps hanging on the outside wall of the cabin. They are the old kind, the ones with sharp points that look like teeth that might snap if you go too close.

The second thing I see makes my heart pound like it wants to jump out of my body and run away. Scattered between the house and the dark bush are small graves like you find in the old graveyard across from the lumberyard. The fenced-in kind. They're made out of logs, just like the cabin, but they're really small, as if made for little children.

"I used to have six. Not much left of their houses, eh?" The old man is standing by the back door. Acimosis is chewing on a bone close by. It doesn't all make sense. He talks to me like we've known each other forever. Like I'm just an old friend that came for a visit. Not someone who has just discovered six little graves in his backyard. I want to run, but my legs won't move.

"Acimosis is the last one, but he never run in a team," the old man says.

Team? That's when I finally get it. *Atim*, of course, is dog. Could *otapewatim* be sled dog? The old man used to have a dog team! I nearly burst out laughing with relief when I find out I'm not looking at graves, but the remains of doghouses.

"Cool!" I say and then I wish I hadn't. The old man looks so forlorn amongst the houses of dogs long gone that it nearly feels like standing in a graveyard.

"*Astam*. Come here." The old man walks into the house, leaving the door wide open. I can't just walk away, so I follow him. It's dark inside and it takes my eyes a while to adjust, but when they do, I blink several times to make sure they are not playing tricks on me.

The cabin is full of stuff like they sell at Poplar Point Trading Post. The stuff you'd think nobody would ever buy anymore. Like oil lanterns and tin coffee pots and barrel stoves and gold-digger pans. It's all here. Okay, maybe not the gold-digger pans, but there are a couple of dark corners I can't really see into. So who knows what all's there. It kind of feels like a museum—except everything in a museum feels so dead. Here it's all still in use.

I sit down on the three-legged stool by the only table in the one-room cabin. The old man throws a couple of teabags into the kettle on the wood stove. The water is already hot, as if he was expecting me. The kettle boils over and water splashes on the hot stove, where it forms tiny little beads that explode into steam. The old man pours tea into a coffee-stained mug and passes it to me. The tea is dark and scummy, and my stomach turns when I take the mug. I spoon heap after heap of sugar into my cup and, when I'm done, something is floating in the swirls my teaspoon leaves behind.

He pushes a piece of bannock across the table.

"No, thanks." That was too quick. I don't want to offend the old man.

"Ehm ... sorry. I just ate." Which is normally not a reason for me to say no to bannock, but this day is turning out to be anything but normal.

The old man sips his tea with loud slurping noises.

"So you had sled dogs? Did you race them?" I ask. I know it's kind of rude. You're not supposed to pester the Elders with questions. Just sit and listen. But it's kind of hard when the old man doesn't say a word. Besides, I really, really want to know about the dogs.

A few years back, when there were still a couple of teams in town, they had dog races at the winter festival. Justin and I used to go to the races down by the lake and watch the teams.

One time, we chased a bunch of loose dogs down to the ice just to see what would happen. The strays barked like crazy and tried nipping at the sled dogs, but the sled dogs just went about their business. All but one team. They chased right after the little guys, and the musher couldn't stop his dogs until they ended up in Mina Dynamite's backyard. And Mina doesn't have her name for no reason. Chased that dog team out of her yard with a broomstick. We missed the races that year, but it was well worth it.

I don't think I ever saw the old man there, though.

"I wasn't much of a racer," the old man takes another sip of his tea. "Did the odd one when I happened to be in town during the races. They were trapline dogs, you know. Not like them fast, skinny ones they have today. They had lots of fur, them olden-day dogs. Like Acimosis."

The old man nods toward the window. Acimosis is curled up outside. His nose is tucked under his tail and fresh snow covers his yellow fur. A cold wind is blowing in from the lake, but Acimosis doesn't seem to mind.

The old man stares out of the window. I'm burning to ask him what it was like to have dogs on the trapline and what happened to all his dogs, but I don't think he's in a talking mood. So we just sit there and drink our tea. I even forget about the floaties.

When the fire burns down, I help him carry wood in. I didn't know there were any houses here that don't have natural gas. They only brought it up here two years ago, but now everyone has it. And before that, we had propane. I can't think of any other houses that have just a wood stove and no electricity, except for the sheds behind people's houses. Justin's older cousin lives in one of those. But he put an extension cord into it, so he can listen to his music and run an electric heater. So I guess it doesn't really count.

"Is Acimosis a sled dog?" I ask when I can't take the long silence any more.

"He never saw a harness in his life. He was just a puppy then, you know."

I know it's just a saying, the old man's "you know," because I sometimes say it myself. Like "eh." But I have this weird feeling that he *does* expect me to know. Know what?

CHAPTER 5

Justin hasn't been in school since our fight at the playground. He isn't exactly the kind of kid you imagine to win the Student of the Month Award for attendance, so I'm not too worried. In a way, I'm kind of relieved, 'cause I wouldn't know what to say to him. Besides, I don't feel like playing video games.

I want to go back to the old man's house and hear more stories about his dog team and see Acimosis. If I wasn't stuck in school, I'd go right now.

We are in the Cree culture room, finishing the snowshoes we started making a few months back. There are pieces of yellow rope on the floor everywhere. I'm done mine and I've got nothing else to do, so I look at the old black and white photographs on the wall. I never paid much attention to them. I mean, they're kind of cool, because they're like historic records of the past. There are women scraping moose hides on big wooden frames, babies in cradleboards, and even some really old ones of families in front of tipis, but I never felt a real connection to them. I thought they were just the kind of pictures that hang in all the schools.

Until today. Because there's one picture of a dog team pulling a toboggan. The man in the picture is out of focus and it's hard to make out his face because it's half-covered by a fur hat. But the dogs are all in focus. They wear heavy leather harnesses that look like horse harnesses, if it wasn't for the pompoms and fancy beadwork on them. But that's not it. Thing is: the lead dog looks just like Acimosis. I ask one of the girls to take a picture of the photograph with her phone and email it to me, so I can print it out later on Mom's computer. I want to show it to the old man.

The printed-out copies of the photograph look pretty decent, considering it's just a cell phone picture from an old black and white photograph. One copy I put in my drawer where I keep my Dad's old hunting knife. Mom gave it to me on my twelfth birthday. The handle is made from a deer foot. It's so tiny, it must be from a fawn. I often touch the deer foot and stroke the hair. I love how smooth and soft it feels and, at the same time, I'm always sad for the deer. I put the photo of the dog team under the knife and, for a second, I get this strange feeling that this is where it belongs.

The knife cover is made of smoke-tanned moose hide with flowers beaded on it. I don't know where my dad got the knife from and, of course, Mom didn't say anything about it, except that Dad would have wanted me to have it. Here's the strange thing: the dog driver in the picture is wearing a moose-hide jacket with beadwork just like on the knife cover. The pattern looks almost the same. Stupid, I think. Of course it looks almost the same. It's the kind of flower design you find on all the moccasins and mitts around here. I close the drawer and take the second photograph with me when I walk over to see the old man.

★

Acimosis comes to greet me as soon as I walk through the gate. His back end wiggles and it looks like his tail almost wags a tiny bit. Is he getting better? Will it ever heal? I wish I could ask someone, but I know that's impossible. I don't think the old man knows what I did and, for sure, I don't want to tell him—or Mom.

Acimosis sniffs my hand. "Sorry, pal, nothing for you today." I ruffle his fur with both hands and he rolls over. When I pet his belly, Acimosis looks like he's smiling. I smile back.

"Thank you, Acimosis," I say. I think he likes me and that makes me feel good.

Acimosis runs around to the back of the cabin but, before he rounds the corner, he stops as if he's waiting for me.

I have to push hard against the old door before it opens wide enough for me to squeeze through. The old man is kneeling by the stove, stoking the fire. He drops one log after the other into the belly of the stove. Slow and deliberate, as if he's got all day to do it. The flames shoot out of the stove, and the stove rattles and roars as if it's trying to get airborne. Cool, I think, but change my mind when I see the stovepipe turning a dark glowing red.

Last year, two houses burned down. I never really thought about how the fires started. There's always some rumor about house fires—like kids playing with matches, electrical fire, a jealous girlfriend. But I can totally see how easy it would be for this old house to catch on fire. The stove is rusty and just about see-through in the center part. The old man turns a damper in the stovepipe and the stove settles down. By the time we sit by the kitchen table, the stove is back to its usual rust color and puts out a nice heat.

I push the photograph across the table. He looks at it a long time. Then he walks over to his bed. He rummages in an old wooden 7Up crate that's storage and night stand at the same time and pulls out a birch bark basket. He doesn't talk to me and I start to wonder if I should leave, but before I can make up my mind, he's back with his tobacco pouch and pipe. It takes a while before it's lit and, all this time, he still doesn't say a word. The tobacco smells sweet and bitter at the same time. The air feels warm and heavy.

"That's an old picture, that one," he says and points with his lips toward the photo on the table.

"So it's not Acimosis?" I ask.

"That picture was taken many winters before Acimosis was born."

"Oh," I say, a bit disappointed, although I know I shouldn't be, because the old man already told me Acimosis had never pulled a sled. It's just that the dog in the photo looks so much like him.

"So when was this picture taken, then?" I ask.

"Long, long time ago. Before there was a road up north. I was just a boy then. We had a trapline way up north past Caribou Narrows."

"The guy in the picture is a trapper?" I ask.

He clicks his tongue and shakes his head. I realize he is about to tell me the story, if only I wouldn't interrupt him.

"We used to stay at the trapline from the time the geese are flying south till the eagle returns. Sometimes we didn't see anybody until Christmas. So Christmas was a special time. The week before Christmas, all the families would start heading to Poplar Point to trade and go to church and gather.

"We were lucky. We had two dog teams. My dad, he had all the fur in the sled and my mom all the kids, and *kohkom*, too.

"We go maybe ten miles and then we have tea. The dogs rest and then we go again. Sometimes we go thirty miles a day. Sometimes twenty. Took us five days to go to Poplar."

"Five days? Where did you sleep?" I bite my tongue. "Sorry."

"There were lots of people living in the bush back then. Not like today. We just go until we come to a cabin and we stay with the families. Sometimes there are other families with their dogs there already. Then the kids sleep under the table or we put the table outside."

"With the kids?"

The old man laughs. "Maybe that would have been a good idea. We haven't seen nobody for so long, we play and talk all night until dad tells us to go to sleep.

"The next day, we go to Pisew Lake. Now, there are maybe five or six teams traveling together."

He draws a trail with his finger through the spilled sugar on the plastic tablecloth.

"This is our trapline. Caribou Narrows is here, and then you take the six-portage route to Pisew. Lots of caribou here."

"You said back then there was no road? How did they get there?"

"There was lots of trails in the bush, way more than today. Those were our roads. All them trapline trails, they were all connected."

The old man draws a big circle on the table—Poplar Lake.

"This here is Fish River. Lots of cabins here." He puts his tea mug down. My mug becomes Poplar Point. He draws the trail in between. It looks easy on the sugar map, but I know there are tons of islands and narrows and peninsulas out there. They all look the same, and you can't tell what is mainland and what is island.

"How do they know the way?"

"They just do. Like you know your way to school. It's all in here." The old man points at his head and I feel a bit stupid, because I can't even begin to imagine how someone can remember a hundred or more miles of trail that isn't really a trail. Just lakes and portages and more lakes. Thinking of being out there in the middle of nowhere without a GPS makes me shiver. What if you were lost or caught in a storm?

"The last day we camp at Fish River. From there, it's only eighteen miles to town. There are so many dog teams now that there's no room for all in the cabins. Us boys, we make a bed of spruce boughs by the fire, but them old trappers, they just crawl into their toboggans. The next morning, we wash up and get our fancy clothes out, and then we race to town.

"Them guys from Caribou Narrows always had good dogs."

I try to picture the loaded toboggans with all their gear and food and furs and kids and dog teams coming from everywhere, all racing toward Poplar Point.

"How fast did they go?" I ask.

"Fast. But not as fast as the race on Christmas day. By that time, all the dogs had a good rest and the sleds were empty. We always traded dogs. So by the time race day comes, everyone has new dogs in their teams. My mom, she was the one who could tell a good dog from a lazy dog. But my dad, he ran the race.

"How…" How long was the race, I was going to ask, but this time I manage to catch myself before I interrupt him again.

"There were maybe thirty families camped around the church and even more dog teams. The store manager, he put out a prize. First one who finishes the thirty-mile loop around Kitsaki Island gets a bag of flour."

"A bag of flour? That's it?" I can't see anyone getting excited about a bag of flour. Imagine we had a fishing derby and, instead of a brand new boat, you get a bag of flour if you win. Nobody would come.

"It was one of them big flour bags. Fifty pounds. Makes lots of bannock. My mom, she make dresses for my sisters from the bag."

The way the old man talks about the flour, I feel kind of embarrassed. That bag of flour must have meant a lot back then.

"People took a lot of pride in their dogs. That year, my dad had the fastest dogs. The priest took that picture here."

"That's your dad? That's so cool! The picture was hanging in my school and I didn't even know."

"He would have liked you," the old man says.

Suddenly I feel as if I'm part of this story. I know it's kind of silly. All I did was pick up an old photo.

CHAPTER 6

"Where were you?" Mom asks as soon as I step through the door. Her hands are pressed into her hips and it doesn't take a genius to figure out she's mad. Real mad. Before I can think of an answer, she points to her computer. The picture of the dog team is up on the screen. I must have forgotten to close it when I left.

"Where did you get this from?" She looks at me like she's the detective and the photo is the evidence that makes me guilty of the crime. Only I have no idea what the crime might be.

"It's from one of the pictures in my school," I tell her.

"How come it's on my computer screen?"

I'm not sure if this is about her computer, which I'm allowed to use for school projects, or if this has something to do with the picture itself.

"It's ... for a school project." I really don't want to lie but, in a way, that's her own fault. Why does she make such a big deal out of it?

"School project?" She raises her eyebrows. So she doesn't believe me. Fine.

"I thought it was the old man in the photo. You know, the one that lives in the old cabin at the end of the road? I made a copy to ask him about it."

"You went to talk to Jack?" Mom sits down on the couch and rubs her forehead as if she has a headache.

"It wasn't him in the picture, anyway," I say quickly, like it would make things better, even though I have no clue what's wrong. Mom knows his name and I wonder what else she knows, but I think it's not a good thing to ask right now.

"What did he say?" Mom's voice sounds kind of flat, like she's real tired or really annoyed.

"Not much," I say, and in a way, that's not a lie. He talked a lot more than on my first two visits but, like before, I felt there was much more unsaid than said.

"What did he say?" Her voice sounds sharp. So I tell her what he told me, but I leave the bits out where we talked about Acimosis and the weird feeling that I somehow should know him—or he somehow knows me.

"That's all?" she asks, like she's surprised or relieved or a bit of both.

"That's it," I say and Mom nods.

"I don't want you to go there anymore."

"What?! Why?" The idea of not going there anymore bothers me more than I would have thought.

"Because he's an old drunk and nothing good ever came from that place. End of discussion."

"He's no drunk," I say. I've been in houses of friends' drunk parents or aunties or cousins, or whatever. The houses reek of booze, and you almost always find an empty or half-empty bottle somewhere. Most often, you don't even have to look very hard. I would have known by the way he talks.

"What do you know?" The way she asks, I know it's one of those questions that requires no answer.

"Okay, I don't know," I say, "but you never complain when I visit Uncle Charlie." I bite my lip as soon as it comes out.

Uncle Charlie is Mom's favorite brother because he used to look out for her when she was young and they lived in the city. Around him, she's still that little girl that needs his protection. Although sometimes I wonder how grown-up he really is.

"At least he hasn't anybody's death on his conscience!"

Mom grabs her coat and runs out the door.

I run after her. "Where are you going?!"

"Making sure that old fart knows he's got no business with you!"

★

It's late at night when Mom comes back. I hear the front door close quietly and I tiptoe into the living room. I feel cold and I think it's not just because I'm in my pj's.

Mom sits slouched down on the couch. I can barely make her out in the dim light shining in from the porch. She looks tired or sad. When she left, I was mad that she'd treated me like a little kid that needed her permission to play with his friends. I had sworn that I wouldn't care what she said, and that I wouldn't let her stop me visiting whoever I want. But now all I want is for her to feel better. I sit next to her and put my arm around her shoulder.

"I won't go there anymore, okay?"

Mom gives me a tired smile. She puts her arm around me and squeezes me tight. It's a while since she hugged me like that and, even though I'm not a kid anymore, it feels good. I lean into her and she asks me, "What were you doing there, anyways?"

I tell her about Yellow Dog and pulling his tail, and the sandwiches I saved for him, and how I thought I had seen

Yellow Dog in the picture at school, and how his name wasn't Yellow Dog at all. The words just bubble out of me non-stop, and I don't know if I make any sense, or if I make things better or worse, but it feels good.

And then Mom laughs. She laughs so hard that her eyes go all teary, and next thing I know, I'm laughing, too, even though I'm not sure what we're laughing about. I'm just relieved to get everything out, and I got this feeling that we'll be friends again.

"So it isn't about Jack, then. It's his dog you want to visit?"

I nod, but I can feel a knot tightening in my throat, because I'm not so sure it's just about the dog anymore. Why is Mom making such a big mystery about the old guy?

"What did he say when you went there?" I ask.

"I didn't go," she says and looks at her hands. "I went to Auntie Ida." That explains why she smells of cigarette smoke. Mom normally doesn't smoke, but when she's over at Ida's place, she always does. It's not like she can't afford her own, 'cause she's got a job at the Community Health Clinic. I think it's

MIRIAM KÖRNER

more like she goes to Auntie's when she's upset, and Auntie's all-time cure is to have a strong coffee and a smoke. Except Mom passes on the coffee and doubles up on smokes.

"When you left, you said the old man killed someone? What was that about?"

"Did I say that?" she asks, like she's surprised. "I don't know. I guess I was just mad. I'm sorry."

"Does that mean I can visit the old ... dog again?"

Mom doesn't reply right away. It's like she, too, is looking straight past the wall like the old man did before.

"Mom?"

"Mhm?"

"Can I go see Yellow Dog again?"

"There are some old soup bones in the freezer. Take 'em for your dog if you like. That's what your dad used to do, you know. Always saved bones for the dogs. It drove me mad. They were perfectly fine soup bones. He really liked dogs, you know. Sometimes I thought he liked them better than people."

It's suddenly so silent in the house that you can hear the fridge kick in with a deep sigh. Mom *never* talks about Dad. It's like he never even existed. I hold my breath, hoping she'll say more, but that's it.

"Promise me one thing, though, okay?"

"Okay," I say, quite unsure of what's coming next.

"Promise me you'll never go into the bush with him, okay?"

"Promise," I say, but I have no clue what it's about.

"And never, ever on your own, either, okay?"

"Why would I want to go into the bush with or without the old man?" I ask, but our conversation is over.

"Promise," is all she says.

So I do.

CHAPTER 7

On my way to see Acimosis, I picture how he will dance around me and sniff my pockets. I imagine how his eyes will go wide with excitement when I pull out the bone I have for him; and how he will run around the yard with his head high, as if he wants to show the whole world his treasure. It's funny how a little thing can make a dog so happy. I like that. And I like how it makes me happy, too.

I whistle to myself and start hopping down the road without even thinking. After a few steps, I suddenly feel embarrassed. What if one of my classmates sees me? I'd get teased for sure. I quickly glance around to make sure nobody witnessed me skipping like a little schoolgirl. Luckily, no one is on the road. Just a gray and white dog pawing a KFC box out of the snow bank.

"Hey, girl, what do you have there?"

The dog looks up just for a second and then she returns her attention to the KFC box. She's tall and skinny. So skinny I can count her ribs. She licks the cardboard box as if it was a bucket of ice cream, but all that's there are the greasy stains from long gone chicken pieces.

"Good luck with that," I say and walk away. I feel guilty when my hand touches the soup bone in my pocket. Well, I tell myself, this one is for Acimosis and he's more than just any dog. But then I think he *was* just any dog not even a couple weeks ago.

I turn around and look at the gray and white dog again. She's now rolling over the KFC box as if she's even trying to get the smell out of the box. That's when I realize she's more white than gray. The gray is just grease and dirt—doggy perfume.

"Come here, girl." I kneel down in the snow and hold the bone out to her. She wags her tail and quickly trots toward me, but then she stops and cowers down as if she expects a beating. I've seen Acimosis do this. Usually, he rolls over and I give him a belly rub.

I don't think she's really scared, just showing me her submission. We learned that in school about wolves. There's always Alpha males and females that boss the others around. In the documentary, we saw there was one female the whole pack picked on. When there was food, she always got to eat last. And she always cowered down like the KFC box dog.

I push the bone toward her and slowly back away.

"It's okay, girl, nobody will hurt you."

She wags her tail just a little bit, as if she's even worried to show me how happy she is. Then she grabs the bone and runs down the road, her head and tail high in the air. She's about the same size as Acimosis. Maybe she has some sled dog breeding in her as well. It's funny how she thinks I'm dominant. She could do me way more harm than the other way round.

Is that what it feels like to have a dog team? Do they think you're their leader? I imagine what it would be like to be the Alpha male. I would look out for everyone and make sure nobody gets picked on.

★

Acimosis runs toward me as soon as I turn into the old man's yard. He sniffs my empty pockets.

"I gave it away. If you'd seen how happy she was, you'd understand. You and her would make a fine team, you know?"

Acimosis tries to stuff his nose in my pocket, as if he didn't believe I didn't bring him a treat. I laugh and ruffle his fur. He jumps up on me and licks my face. Sometimes you don't even need a bone to make a dog happy.

★

The photocopy of the old photograph is nailed above the old man's bed. It's the only decorative thing hanging on the wall, if you don't count the pots and pans and the old washbasin dangling from nails near the kitchen cupboard. He sees me glancing at the picture.

"Some nice dogs, those ones, eh?"

I wonder what it would be like to be pulled by a dog team. How would you even make them go?

"I like the one that looks like Acimosis," I say.

The old man puts two teacups on the table. I'm really not keen on tea—scummy or not—but I have the feeling there will be no story without tea. He pours water from an old galvanized pail into the kettle, but there's barely more than a dribble in the pail. The old man puts the empty pail in front of me and grabs another on his way out the door. I grab the pail and follow.

His water tank must be empty or his water lines frozen. I'm preparing myself for the embarrassing knock on the neighbors' door to ask for water. Mom always used to make me go ask for water when ours froze, but since we put extra insulation into the crawlspace, we don't have that problem with freezing water lines anymore. The old man is not going to the neighbors, though. He walks down a well-trodden trail past the doghouse graveyard and into the bush.

The bush. Oh-oh. The forest is dense and the spruce trees look spooky, with the stringy green lichen hanging from the branches like bad Halloween decorations. Acimosis appears and disappears between the trees like a ghostly yellow wolf. Where is the old man going? I'm freaking out and I know I'm totally doing it to myself. Or not quite. In a way, it's Mom's fault, with that weird promise of hers.

Acimosis runs up to me like he's asking me if I'm coming. I bend down to pet him and almost instantly feel calmer.

The old man returns, carrying a full water pail. I feel totally and utterly stupid. He just went down to the lake to get water. Duh! He can't have running water in his cabin. It's built low to the ground, no space for a water tank. And he's got no sink, either; that's why he's got all the old washbasins.

Suddenly it's just a beautiful winter day, the sun glittering through the trees and reflecting off the lake like a million tiny stars. I hurry to fill up my own pail. At first I don't even see the waterhole. There's an old rusty ice-chisel and a pile of snow. When I kick around in the snow, my feet hit something hard. It's like a trapdoor down into the lake. A piece of blue Styrofoam insulation is sandwiched between two sheets of plywood. I get it. It's so the hole won't freeze or, at least, not so fast. When I dunk my pail into the hole, the cold water stings on my hands like a thousand needles.

I hurry back to the cabin. I never thought I'd be so happy to hold onto a cup of warm tea. The old man lights his pipe and stares at the photograph for a while.

"That dog was one heck of a good dog. Worked as hard as two dogs. Smart, too. In the olden days, them toboggans had no brakes, you know. Just tell that dog to stop and he lies down like someone shot him. Wouldn't move until you tell him go again. You could go and check your traps or pull your net, and him, he just sit there. Was my father's pride, that one."

"Not all dogs listened?" I ask.

"Not like your leader. That one is always special. If you have a good dog like that, you want many, many dogs from that one. His bloodline is all over the north. His pups were trapline dogs and freight dogs and, later, racing dogs. One of his grandchildren won that big race in The Pas, world champion dog." The old man smiles like he just won the world championship himself. "One heck of a dog. TwoDog. That's what he called him. Never had one like him again."

I always pictured sled dogs to be just some way of transportation in the past, like skidoos and trucks today. But I never hear anybody talk like that about their snow machines or vehicles—except maybe Leon's older brother. He calls his truck "Babe," even though it's so old and rusty that "Grandma" would have been a more fitting name. But that's not the same. When your truck breaks down or runs out of fuel, you just ditch it and hitch a ride back to town. Back then, they only had their dogs, and probably nobody would come along and ask if they needed a ride. But then again, they probably never broke down with a dog team, either.

"Is Acimosis one of his grandchildren?"

"No, no. TwoDog goes back, lots further back than that. But Acimosis is a throwback to that old line. Him and his dad look just like TwoDog."

"What was his dad's name?"

"Osāwāw."

"Yellow … Yellow Dog?" Is that how you would translate it? I'm all excited, because that's exactly the name I had given Acimosis.

"Yellow One." The old man looks out the window. Acimosis is curled up against the cabin wall. "He's the last one of that line. Nobody wants them olden dogs anymore."

"Why?" It makes me sad to think that Acimosis is the last of his kind. I wonder if he knows he's the last one, but then I think that's really stupid. Two weeks ago, Acimosis was just some dog, and why should I care about his history and what his great-great-great-great-great-grandfather did? Strange thing is, though, I do.

And it's not just Acimosis. All of a sudden, I understand

there's just no more dogs like him, 'cause there aren't any old guys like the old man out there anymore. Trapping and fishing by dog team and all that. Everyone uses a skidoo today. In school, we learn that there were dog teams before skidoos, but they don't tell you what it's like to have a dog team that's real special. And that's when I get the idea.

"You ran dogs, too, right?" I ask.

"Since I was nine years old." He leans back against the cabin wall and stares out the window.

I want to ask him if he still has his sled and harnesses, and if he thinks I could train a dog team, but I can tell his thoughts are elsewhere. So I just wait for another one of his stories. Even though I'm so excited about the possibility of running dogs that I can barely sit still.

"We didn't live in town all year round when I was young, you know."

"I know. You lived on the trapline," I say, but then I realize he knows that I know that. It's just his way of starting a story.

"Every fall we'd load the old canvas canoe till it barely floated. My father sat in the back. My mother sat in the middle on the flour sacks with my sisters, and I sat in the front. My job was to make sure the puppies don't move. The motor could barely push all that load, but we always got there."

"What about the adult dogs—were they in the boat, too?"

"Sometimes, if Dad had a special leader, he would be allowed in the boat. The others ran along the shore.

"I looked after the dogs. They were happy to be with us after the summer on Dog Island."

"Dog Island?"

"That big one in front of town. That's where we left them for the summer. Just went there every couple days to bring them some fish."

A million questions spin in my head, but I know this story is not about Dog Island, so I stay quiet.

"I had a favorite dog back then. My dad called him Bowl Cleaner."

"Bowl Cleaner?" I ask.

"He was no good as a leader. Kind of lazy, too. Ate for three dogs, pulled only for one.

"One night, we wake up and all the dogs are barking. There's something in the smoke tent.

"'I'll be damned if that's not a bear,' says my dad and grabs his rifle. They always come in the fall along the lakeshore, looking for food to fatten up for the winter. Us kids watched from the cabin window. The bear runs toward my dad and throws his paws up on his shoulder. My sisters scream, because they think the bear will kill him now. But my dad, he is laughing. It wasn't a bear. It was Bowl Cleaner. We laughed so hard that he got away without a licken. That time, anyways."

I try to imagine what it would have been like to live in the middle of nowhere in a one-room cabin, just like this one here, except there would be nobody else around for miles and miles. No grocery store. No school. I can't make up my mind if this would have been a dream come true or the worst nightmare ever. Catching lots of fish—that'd definitely be cool. But dealing with all the guts, and hands stinking of fish, and then hanging the fish over a fire and watch them shrivel up and dry … a nightmare. Although I do love the taste of smoked fish.

I think I would have liked the dog part if they were all dogs like Acimosis. Big, but really kind. Acimosis looks at me like he can see right inside me. Cool thing is, he doesn't seem to mind what he's seeing, and that makes me feel good about myself. It's like I could tell him anything, even the mean things I did— like pulling his tail or calling my little cousin "Beaver Face" one time because of her big front teeth—and he would still like me.

"Tell me about running the dogs," I ask the old man.

"When the lake started to freeze, Dad set traps close by, so we can go there on foot. I snared rabbits for stew. My mother and sisters scraped moose hide to make new wrap-arounds for the winter. The dogs would watch our comings and goings and sleep a lot. But as soon as the snow falls, the dogs howl and bark and are restless all day."

"Why? Do they know that they would be hooked up soon? Do they like it?"

"Do they like it? They can't wait. That's what they are bred for. For the love of running.

"That year, I was even more impatient than the dogs. My father had promised me my own trapline. In the fall, I helped him make a toboggan. The same like his, only smaller."

"How did you make it?"

"If you listen, you find out." The old man takes another sip of tea.

Stop being so impatient, I tell myself. But there is so much I want to know.

"To make a toboggan," the old man continues, "we had to walk far to find a birch tree that was big and straight. Back then, we didn't have no chainsaw, you know. My father cut it down with his axe and then he split it into boards with wooden wedges. Lots of work. But not like scraping and tanning the hide. I was glad I was a boy, and sometimes I think my sister wished she was, too. She was a lot better with the axe than with the sewing needle. But that is a different story.

"We boiled the boards to make them soft and bended the front around a tree to make the curl. We used *babiche* to tie them in place. That was my first sled. Bowl Cleaner and TwoDog made my first dog team."

"TwoDog? He was your dog?"

"When he was too young to run in the big team. I trained Bowl Cleaner and TwoDog in their first winter. I tied them to my little toboggan and sat my youngest sister on it. I ran ahead and they followed me. My sister loved it.

"One day, we were up on the big hill when the dogs back home started barking. The kind of bark they do at feeding time. Bowl Cleaner and TwoDog take off so fast that my sister falls off the sled. A rope catches on her leg and she drags behind the dogs all the way home. Her skirts and even her underwear was full of snow. She screamed so loud that my mother came out and gave me a good slap. But I didn't even mind because

I knew then that Bowl Cleaner and TwoDog would be good, strong dogs."

The old man smiles so wide that I can see that little boy in him. We both laugh as if the story had just happened.

★

I listen to the old man's stories about setting up his own trapline, snaring rabbits, catching his first lynx, skinning animals, and preparing the hides for sale, but all I really want to know is about the dogs.

My favorite story is the one where he was caught in a snowstorm. He had made a fire to sit out the storm. It was late—way past Bowl Cleaner's suppertime—and the dog became restless. The old man crawled into his toboggan and fell asleep. A sudden jerk woke him up, and there was Bowl Cleaner pulling the sleeping boy along. Even TwoDog couldn't stop him. Bowl Cleaner ran all the way home before the old man could even get out of his sleeping bag and climb on the running board. When the old man's father opened the cabin door, Bowl Cleaner burst inside. He would have went right for the stew pot on the stove had his mother not tackled the dog and dragged him outside.

At first I wasn't sure if that's just a story, because the old man said there was lots of fresh snow and he couldn't find his old trail, so I didn't know if a dog could. But then he tells me how the dogs find the portages between the lakes after a whole season has gone by, and even stop at the spots where the traps were set the year before; and how they always find their way back, even if the dog driver is lost.

I sit there and listen to story after story until it's pitch-black outside. The more he talks, the more I want to be that boy he's talking about. I don't even care if I have to clean fish and bring in firewood and all that, because I would get to sit by the warm stove at night and slurp my bowl of soup or stew and think about all the cool adventures I had with my dogs.

★

"Do you still have your sled and harnesses and all that stuff?"

"Let's see," he says and grabs the old oil lamp.

Behind the house, there's a shed that looks even older than the log cabin. It's got poles for a roof, and strips of blue tarp are hanging down the sides. The weight of the snow on the roof is threatening to collapse the whole building, and I'd rather not go in.

But when the old man starts rummaging in the shed and the light shines on a wooden toboggan, I just have to go and see it. The old man shuffles a fishnet out of the way and pulls a pair of snowshoes out of the sled bag—or at least I assume it was a sled bag at some time. It's black with mold and looks like mice chewed bits and pieces out of it for their nests.

The snowshoes are homemade with real rawhide webbing instead of yellow rope. The fishnet has wood floats and rocks for weights, and there's even a canvas canoe hanging under the ceiling. The kind with wooden ribs that you only see in really old pictures.

MIRIAM KÖRNER

"Grab that," the old man says, and I hurry to help him lift a wooden box out of the toboggan. I pry the lid open.

The box is filled with dog harnesses! My heart is pounding like crazy. There are at least six or seven leather harnesses. Surely one of them must fit Acimosis. Would the old man let me run him?

I take out the harnesses and underneath are tiny leather moccasins, like you see on babies. Lots and lots of them. I pick one up and it smells smoky, like home-tanned hide, but there's another smell, too. Like stinky socks, only sweeter.

"For when the ice is rough and sharp in the springtime. It cuts up their paws, so we put these moccasins on them."

"These are dog booties? Cool!"

I've seen them on dogs at the Canadian Classic Dog Sled Race—that 150-mile race that goes all the way from Prince Albert to Poplar Point and back. But those booties are all made of fabric with really crazy colors, like neon green.

Once there was a racer who came to our school with her

sled dogs. She let us put the booties on the dogs and harness them, but the harnesses looked a lot different as well. They didn't have such heavy collars as these leather ones. There weren't many kids keen on harnessing the dogs. The younger kids were mostly scared, but we all wanted to stand on the sled and run the dogs. Only three were allowed to climb into her sled when she ran a loop around the schoolyard. I wasn't one of them. How cool would it be if I could run a dog team all on my own?

"Can we hook up Acimosis to your sled?"

The old man takes the booties out of my hand and puts them back into the box. He shuts the lid and piles the net and other stuff on top of the box, as if he wants to bury it. I start to wonder if he has heard my question.

"Your mom would not be happy. There is no use for all this old stuff anymore. I should have burned it a long time ago."

I feel like a door has been slammed shut. So much for my idea of starting my own dog team. I don't follow the old man back to the cabin. I don't think he's going to tell more stories, and I don't feel like listening to any more right now.

★

I have barely left the yard when the white and gray KFC box dog comes running toward me. Her paws hardly touch the ground—she moves like a dancer. When she gets close, she cowers down like before, but this time she seems a little less shy. I walk away without looking at her. I feel a sting in my throat. I shouldn't have given her the bone, shouldn't have dreamt about having a dog team. I am almost down the road before I can't take it any longer. I stop and look back. She's still standing on the road where I left her. She's looking at me as if she expects me to come back.

Why can't I use his old dog stuff?

CHAPTER

I suddenly find myself on Lynx Road. I don't know why I don't turn at Bear Place to go home.

Or maybe I do know. When I left the old man, I wanted to talk to Mom right away and ask her what the old man knows about us and why she doesn't trust him. The only thing is, I can already tell you the end of the conversation. If she doesn't want to talk about something, she'll just ignore it. "How do I know what he knows about us?" And: "Who said I don't trust him?" She always wins.

It's not worth it. Plus, Saturday morning is Mom's laundry day. Our washing machine broke down a couple of months ago and we have a new one on order, but the model she picked out of the Sears catalogue is on back order.

So we have to go to the laundromat. There's only one in town, and they're so busy with washing laundry for the uranium mines, that you sometimes have to wait for hours to get your stuff into a machine that isn't broken. Dryers are worse. I've been there so often that I know which ones are still drying hot and which ones aren't drying at all.

There's one I call the Jackpot. It runs forever. But it's hardly ever free. I guess I'm not the only one who knows the dryers. Point is: until we get our washing machine back, I don't like being in the vicinity of Mom on Saturday mornings, 'cause guess who's going to sit there and watch dirty socks tumble around in circles while Mom runs around and does the shopping?

But I know that's only part of the reason why I end up on Lynx Road. Justin hasn't been in school all week and, although I didn't really want to see him, I kept looking for him. I'm not sure why. I guess it's just kind of boring without him. I also feel bad about the fight we had at the playground. I just don't know what to do about it. When I pulled Acimosis's tail, it only took a couple of sandwiches and bones to make things better. Why does it have to be so much more complicated with humans?

Maybe it *is* as simple as that! I run back home as fast as I can and grab my skates and hockey sticks. Justin's stick broke on the first game we played this season. It was old, but he also hit the goal post pretty hard when the other team scored. It wasn't even a real game, just Justin and me against a couple of other boys. He hasn't played since. Obviously. But I got a second stick since. My mom bought it for me when she saw me fiddling around with it at True Value last week. Nothing fancy, but a lot nicer than my old one.

Justin's house is the second one from the school on Lynx Road. Although I hang out there a lot, because Justin's older brother has an Xbox, I don't really like going there. His dad always talks to me like I'm his buddy, which is all right, I guess. But sometimes he says weird stuff to me. One day, when Justin was right there, his dad said that he wished Justin was as smart and good looking as I was. I always pretend I don't hear him, because I don't know what to say. Justin tries really hard to please him, but his dad always finds something wrong.

Today, I'm especially not up to facing his dad, so I walk around the side of the house and knock on Justin's window. The broken half is fixed up with a piece of plywood. I peek through the glass side but don't see him there. I slide the window open and push my hockey stick through the opening. Justin will know who it came from because a few years ago, he wrote *Justin Rules* on my stick and, even though I tried to rub it off, it's still there.

I walk over to the rink behind the school. Nobody's there. The rink hasn't been cleared since the new snow, but there's a half-broken snow shovel leaning against the fence. I don't have anything better to do, so I clear the ice. I skate as fast as I can, round and round and round. The cold air washes over my face. It feels sharp and prickly, but in a good way. I pick up my stick and push the puck over the ice. With each shot, I think of how I can make things better between Justin and me.

"About the other day, man. Look, I'm sorry I hit you. But that stuff with the dog, that was really messed up."

The puck bounces off the goal post.

"Hey, what's going on? You know you can talk to me, right?"

This time the puck flies right over the goal into the deep snow. I sound like the school social worker.

"Looks like you need a good beating."

I freeze when I hear Justin's voice, which is kind of stupid when you're on skates, because I just keep going until I hit the edge of the rink. Justin laughs when I fall into the snow bank face first.

"Giving up already?"

"Look, I don't want to ..." I was going to say fight, but then I see that Justin is putting on his skates. I feel stupid.

"Don't want what? To lose?" Justin grins.

"Right. Like that's gonna happen."

I hit the puck hard; it slides across the ice and into the goal on the other side. I know I'm the better player, and Justin knows it, too.

But he plays hard. Harder than I've ever seen him play before. We skate, score, wrestle, and then do it all over again until it's pitch-black. The score is 18:18 and, although we still skate hard, nobody gets another goal.

"Time out!" I call and flop onto the ice. I lie on my back with my arms spread out like wings. There's no moon yet and the stars look really bright.

"Hey, there's a shooting star! Make a wish!"

It just came without thinking. My mom used to say it to me when I was little, and I always, always made a wish. I still do, even though I know it's stupid and they never come true, but I guess I don't want to miss my chance, in case this one was the one. So I make my wish. Justin sits next to me.

"Do you ever wonder what's out there?" he asks. "Sometimes I wish I could be a star, a little light in the dark, and nobody could ever reach me."

I don't know what to say and, before I can think of something, the moment has passed.

"Are you giving up or are we gonna finish this game?" Justin gives me a shove with his elbow.

I stand up and lean on my stick. "Next goal wins!"

We start playing again. But it's a lot softer than before. It's almost like each of us hopes the other one scores. I am skating toward the goal when I see a dog out of the corner of my eye. It's the gray and white one I'd given the bone to before. I shoot and throw up my arms.

"Game over." I glance at Justin, hoping he doesn't see her. But he does.

"Hey!" he yells and raises his stick. "Sneaking up on me like a wolf! I'll show you!"

"Wait!" I say and grab his stick. "She's okay. She's with me."

"She? You know that dog?"

"She's my lead dog. Or, at least, I hope she's going to be. I … I'm getting a dog team. Like … remember the races we used to watch? That's what I want to do. Run dogs. There used to be a lot of sled dogs here in the past, and I bet half the dogs running around loose now have some sort of sled dog blood in them. So I'll get myself a team, maybe four or five to start with."

"What?!" Justin looks at me as if I'd told him I just launched a rocket to Mars.

To be honest, I'm just as surprised as he is. I didn't even know it was that important to me. But now that I've said it out loud, it sounds totally right.

"When did you get that idea?"

"I … I don't know … just now, I guess."

I'm not ready to tell him about Acimosis and the old guy and, in a way, it's kind of the truth. I never thought about KFC box dog being on my team before, or even about having my own team. I look at the dog and she looks back at me and wags her tail. Justin laughs, but his eyes don't.

"All right then. Where's your … what do you call the thing you put on the dogs?"

"Harness?"

"Yeah, where's your harness? Let's harness her up and see if she can pull."

"I don't have one."

"Let's get some rope." Justin breaks a willow. "I got the whip."

The dog cowers down when she hears the willow snap and slinks away from us.

Justin smiles. I feel my mouth turn dry. This is not good.

"I'm serious, Justin. I want to do this. I mean, really do this. Get myself a sled and some harnesses and … I don't know if I need a whip."

"Serious? You want to be a dog driver? Like the guy in *White Fang*—or what's that stupid movie called?"

"*White Fang.*" I'm surprised that Justin knows about it. I got the book from the school library. It was the only one I could find on sled dogs. It's really old and kind of hard to read, but it gets you inside the wolf-dog's head and that's pretty sweet. I for sure hope Happy here is easier to tame than White Fang. Happy. I like that name.

"Happy!" I say to the dog just to see how it sounds. Happy

wags her tail.

"What?" Justin asks.

"Her name is Happy," I explain.

"The only time you'll see her happy is when she's got a piece of your butt in her jaws. And the only time you'll see me happy is when she's at least a mile away." Justin raises his willow.

"LEAVE HER ALONE!" I say, louder than I meant to.

"Then go and talk to that stupid dog!" Justin throws the hockey stick I wanted him to have into the bush.

"Have yourself a nice life," he says and leaves.

I stay and think about our conversation. Why is he so ticked off? So what if it's not his thing? He still doesn't need to be upset with me. Happy comes within reach and I kneel down to pet her. She rubs against me and wags her tail so hard that it sounds like a drumbeat on my legs.

I laugh and feel better right away. Happy follows me as I walk home.

"Wait here, okay?" I say as I walk up the steps to our front door. Happy puts her ears back; she crouches down and wags her tail that's squeezed in between her legs. It's almost as if she turns all shy whenever I talk to her directly. As if she's not sure if it's okay to wag her tail—or as if she's not sure she can trust me being her friend again.

Mom's watching the news when I come in. I go straight to the fridge and pile a bunch of leftovers on a plate. I sneak into my room and call Happy from the open window. She does her shy tail wag, but doesn't dare come into our yard. I chuck a piece of pork chop out the window. She quickly grabs it and runs back to the road where she gobbles it down. The next piece she eats right under the window.

"That's a good girl," I say. "You can come back anytime, you know?"

I talk to her through the window until she curls up tight against the wall. My bed is just on the other side. Just before I fall asleep, I hear her leave. I think about how little it takes to befriend a dog, and how little it takes to lose a human friend.

MIRIAM KÖRNER

CHAPTER 9

It's Saturday and, even though it's a nice day outside, I'm going to the library. I want to know how to make a dog harness, and the easiest way to find out is to use the free high-speed Internet at the library. I know I don't have a dog, but since I told Justin last Saturday I'm going to have a dog team, I can't think of anything else. Not that he would care. We haven't talked since our fight and I haven't been over to see the old man. If I can't use his harnesses, I'll make my own. Maybe I can try it out on Happy.

I'm halfway to the library when I see a white dog with a chip bag.

It's funny how the way I see has changed since I got interested in the dogs. Whenever I see something move, I look to see if it's a dog. If it's white, I get all excited, but most of the times, it's not Happy. I'm surprised how many dogs are roaming the streets. Did I not notice them before, or are they moving around more now that it's winter and food is not so easy to find?

This time the white dog is Happy—the chip bag is the dead giveaway. I look down the street to see if someone's there who could be her owner, but, as always, she's on her own.

"Hey, Happy!" I call. She immediately turns her head, and it's almost as if she smiles when she recognizes me. I pet her for a bit and then ask her if she'd like to be a sled dog. She does her shy little tail wag. A careful maybe? Or maybe she didn't understand the question.

"Think about it," I say as I turn to go into the library. "We can figure it out together."

★

Happy is sitting by the library door when I come back out with my harness measurements written on a piece of scrap paper. She must have waited for me the whole time I was at the computers. It took a little longer because I changed the screen to a game whenever someone I knew walked by, and then I ended up playing a bit. And then there were so many different kinds of harnesses. Some were even knitted with wool in all sorts of colors. But those were just for fancy little lap dogs. I like the old-style harness the old man has. They're really heavy-duty moose hide ones with a stiff collar that has wire inside and is made to fit each dog. But I can't make those. Moose hide is hard to come by and really expensive if you buy it at the Trading Post. Finally, I found a pattern for a sled dog harness made with webbing. I wrote down how to measure the dog and all the steps to sew the harness together.

"Hey, Happy!" I say as she walks up to me. I say it real quietly and don't look at her, because there are lots of people on the street. It makes me kind of happy that she follows me, and probably nobody is going to miss her, but I still feel a bit guilty. She may be someone's dog. She's got no collar, but that doesn't mean anything. Half the dogs don't have collars.

"You can go wherever you want, okay?" I say. She runs ahead and then stuffs her head into the snow bank. She digs frantically and then pulls out an empty chip bag. I wonder if it's the same one and she just buried it like other dogs bury bones. Happy looks at me as if she's saying, "Look what I found." She puts her paw inside the bag and then rips it open with her mouth. She licks the salt like it's the best thing ever. I laugh as I walk by her. Happy picks up her bag, runs ahead, and starts all over again.

"I'll get you some more," I say. I stop by Andy's gas bar. I grab a BBQ-flavored bag and finger the change out of my pocket. Then my eyes fall onto the beef jerky and I change my mind. I trade chips for jerky and hand my money to the cashier.

"That's it?" he asks.

I nod, but then I got an even better idea. "Wait! You got any dog food?"

"That's your dog? Tell him to get out of my garbage can."

I look out the window and see Happy pulling out pieces of

garbage. Ever so carefully, she drops them to the ground and sniffs them. Then she picks another one.

"Uhmm ... no, she isn't mine. No idea where she came from. You?"

"Thought he was yours. It's about time they have another dog-shooting day—them stray ones are starting to run around in packs."

I feel the blood rush into my ears and hear my heart throbbing in my head. Dog-shooting day! It's all good and fine to have Happy follow me as she pleases, but she can't be loose on dog shooting day. Whenever that might be. I nearly forget to pay for the jerky. I'm suddenly in such a rush.

"Come, Happy!"

Happy leaves an ice cream wrapper and follows me. I run down the street. I have this horrible feeling I have to do something real quick to keep Happy safe, but I don't know what to do. Suddenly I feel ridiculous, having wasted my day in the library, looking up harnesses and dreaming of being a musher.

CHAPTER 10

"Why can't I keep her?" I put my best pleading face on, but I'm not doing a good enough job, 'cause Mom doesn't budge.

"You don't even have a dog house for it. And how are you going to pay for dog food? Besides, you don't even know where it came from. Maybe some little kid is missing it right now!"

"She!"

"She? It belongs to a she? Whose dog is it, then?"

"No, Mom. Happy is a she. I don't know who she belongs to."

"How do you know she's called Happy, then?" Mom stems her hands on her hips. It's hopeless.

"Never mind. I'll find a place for her."

I leave the supper table, even though I know Mom has blueberry pie for dessert.

"Before you run out the door, what happened to the jeans in the garbage?"

"They were old and holey, so I cut 'em up."

"Cut 'em up?"

"I made a harness. For Happy."

"You made what? No, no, no! Don't even think of it! You are not going back to Jack if he's putting ideas in your head."

"He's not!" I'm getting really upset now. "Doesn't even let me touch his dog stuff—like something bad will happen! I like dogs, Mom! What's so wrong about that?"

I'm so mad now that I don't even wait for a reply. I grab the harness I started making and leave. I can feel the house shake when I slam the front door. This whole sled dog thing is not going to work, anyway. Happy wiggled away and twisted and turned every time I tried to put the harness on her. Plus, how am I going to train her if I have to find her somewhere on the streets every time I want to work with her? Never mind that I don't even have a sled. I throw Happy's harness into the garbage can. Happy runs around me, her tail wagging wildly.

"Go home!" I yell.

Her tail disappears between her legs and she hunkers down, as if someone had just hit her with a stick. She whines softly. Almost like a child crying silently to herself.

"Sorry, Happy, so sorry. Come here, girl. It's not your fault."

She licks my hand and I feel my throat tightening. I'm so scared I might lose her that I wish I never had met her.

I don't think she's got a home, which I kind of hoped at first, because then there was a chance she could become my dog. Now I just wish someone would look out for her. It could have been so easy. Why doesn't Mom let me have Happy? My dad liked dogs, she said. I wish he were here right now. Maybe he'd understand how I feel. Maybe he'd help me.

Happy nudges me with her nose and licks my ear, as if she's trying to make me feel better.

"I'm okay, girl," I rub her head. "But I'm worried about you. We have to find a home for you, okay?"

Happy walks quickly to the garbage can, like she's on a mission. Her whole head disappears in the can, and when she reappears, she has the jean harness in her mouth.

"What now?" I ask her. "First you made such a fuss when I tried to put it on and now you want it?" She drops the harness by my feet. I pick it up. I think about who I could ask to keep Happy for me, but there's only one person I can think of.

★

There's a faint light shining through the plastic-covered window of the old log cabin. It looks warm and cozy, not at all like the bright electric lights in our house. Acimosis comes rushing out of his barrel. When he sees Happy, the hair on his neck stands up and he looks even bigger. Happy crawls up to him and licks his face. Acimosis sniffs Happy and then he wags his tail.

"Acimosis! Your tail! You can wag your tail again."

The dogs must sense the excitement in my voice. Acimosis jumps up on me and then Happy, too, as if she's imitating her new friend. We stand for a little while in a kind of awkward hug until Acimosis walks to the back door, like he's done the last few times I came to visit. I'm not sure if I'm ready to go in. I don't know what to say. Or better: I don't know what to do if he says, "No."

★

"Jeremy!" The old man gets up from his bed. "*Tansi*," he nods in greeting, and then his eyes wander to the kettle. I fill it up and put it on the stove. Then I take a stick from the big pile of logs next to the door and stoke the fire.

"Storm's coming," the old man says. "It's gonna get cold. Hear the lake making ice?"

I listen to the wind howling through the trees but I don't hear the ice. When I was a kid, I often lay awake at night trying not to listen to the eerie sound. Now I don't mind it anymore.

It's still eerie, but also beautiful. Like a sad song. It makes you want to cry, but you can't stop listening.

I try hard to listen beyond the whistling of the kettle and the wind in the trees, but all I can hear is dogs howling in the distance. And then Acimosis and Happy join in. Acimosis has a deep howl, long and sad. Happy's is kind of yappy. Like she doesn't know if she wants to howl or bark. I guess you could say she's a bad howler. Can't really keep the tune.

"Whose dog?" the old man asks. I take a deep breath and then I let it out.

"That's Happy. She … she's been following me around and … I really like her, but I can't keep her. So I thought, maybe we can fix up one of the old dog houses and she can stay here?"

The old man doesn't say a word. I feel like at school when the teacher returns a math test. You've done all you could do, can't change anything, but you don't know if you've passed until the teacher slams it on your desk. I feel my hands getting sweaty and I fiddle with the harness.

The old man reaches across the table and takes the harness. His hands glide, careful, across the material and he rubs his fingers across my stitches. The way he treats it, like it's something special, makes me proud and embarrassed at the same time. It's a harness, all right, but the edges are fraying already, and my stitches show that I didn't exactly pay attention when Mrs. Ratt taught us how to sew moccasins.

The old man nods his head and looks at me with a different kind of look. For the first time, he's really looking at me. I feel like a long conversation has passed between us, only not a word was exchanged, and I'm not exactly sure what the topic was.

"What does your mother say?"

"She ..." I want to say she's cool with it, but I know she's not, and even though I really want the old man to keep Happy, I can't lie to him. "She'll get used to it. She always lets me do my thing in the end."

The old man nods thoughtfully.

"And I don't have a dad," I add, even though I have the

feeling he knows. "He died when I was three." The old man nods again.

"You know what happened?"

"To my dad? Not really. Only that it was an accident. It wasn't his fault. Someone else caused it. I never asked my mom about the details, because she doesn't like talking about Dad." I take a sip of my tea and then I ask the question I've been wondering about for a while. "Did you know my dad?"

"Yes," he says, simple as that. And then he says no more. I want to ask how and when and what was he like, but I don't. I guess I'm scared of the answer. Maybe it's easier not to know, not to have a picture of him in my head, not to wish I could have met him. Not to miss him.

"So you want to be a dog driver?" The old man interrupts the awkward silence and pushes the harness back across the table. "Do you know how to build a fire?" he asks.

"Kind of," I say. I don't want to tell him that Justin and I have lots of practice lighting fires. We like to burn old mattresses at the dump. The foam kind. It's really neat to see how quick that mattress bursts into flames. Kind of scary, too, if you think of all the stories you hear about someone smoking in bed and then falling asleep.

But I don't think that's what the old man had in mind when he asked me if I knew how to build a fire. I don't know what that's got to do with dog mushing, anyway.

"If you don't know how to build a fire in the bush, you got no business out there. You get cold or wet and don't know how to warm up, that's it."

He rummages for his pipe and I know he's getting ready to tell a story. All I want to know is if I can keep Happy, but I know there's no sense in rushing him. At least he hasn't said, "No," so there's hope.

The old man lights his pipe. "One day, when I was your age, maybe a little older—or a lot, I don't remember—I went to check my traps. By that time, I had a long line. Maybe half a day out and half a day back. The day before, I had seen lynx tracks near one of my far traps and I wanted to see if he'd gone in. 'Gonna storm,' my father had said. 'Go tomorrow.'

"But I didn't listen. Lynx was lots of money at that time and I was saving for a new rifle. So I went. The storm was bad. Lots and lots of snow. The dogs had no trail to follow, so I had to snowshoe. You know how you get hot when you walk in snowshoes?"

I've only ever worn snowshoes when we had races at the school, but they were pretty short. I nod anyways. I know by now, it doesn't really matter what I say. He's in his story.

"I took my mitts off and put them on the sled. Then my fur hat. Even my jacket. Still, I got wet from all the hard work and the snow. Bowl Cleaner kept stepping on my snowshoes, so finally I cut a long stick and tied it to the front of the sled. Keep the dogs stretched out and away from my snowshoes. Gee pole. That's what we used to call it.

"Night came and I was still walking. And then the snow stopped and it got cold. Real cold. No more clouds to keep the warmth. And I couldn't walk no more. I put my jacket back on and my fur hat, but I could only find one mitt. By now, I'm shaking with cold and I know this is bad."

"So what did you do?" I bite my tongue. Obviously, he was just about to tell me and I interrupted him again.

"I go to shore and dig out a spot to build a fire. Use my snowshoe for a shovel. I always have some birch bark in my pocket, but this time I don't need it. There's lots of loose bark on the birches and old man's beard hanging from the spruce. The snow is heavy and wet, so I pick dead branches from the bottom of the trees, where it's dry.

"When my fire is all ready to go, I get out the matches but my hand is so cold, I drop them in the snow. Never drop your matches. It's no good when they are wet. I pick them up as good as I can, and then I warm my hands in Bowl Cleaner's armpits. Nice and warm there, but if you are cold on your body, your hands don't warm up very good. The first match falls out of my hand. The second one I hold on as tight as I can and it breaks. The next one is blown out by the wind.

"Only one match left. I know I am in trouble, but the last match lights good and I hold it to the birch bark. I soon have a nice fire. I was very lucky. My father taught me well and the fire saved my life."

The old man gets up from his chair and rummages in his bedside 7Up crate. He puts a small tin box on the table. Inside is a bit of birch bark and a flint.

"Sometimes, you don't have matches. Then things get bad very quickly. You take this. When you know how to build a fire, you come back."

I close the box and put it into my pocket. I have no idea how to make a fire with flint, but I'm sure I can figure that out. Besides, I'm not worried about building fires. I just want to run dogs around town or on the lake, and not to some faraway trapline. But for now, all I care about is finding a safe place for Happy.

"What about Happy? Can she stay?"

"There's a snow shovel by the door. You can dig one of them old houses out. Maybe there's a piece of plywood in the shed. Maybe not. Then you just make a roof with spruce boughs for tonight. Tomorrow you can cut some grass for her bed and help me set the net."

"Set the net?"

"Catch some dog food."

"Okay," I say, but suddenly I'm overwhelmed. How do you build a doghouse roof with spruce boughs, find grass in the winter, and set a net under the ice?

Luckily, I do find an old sheet of plywood. I nail it to the house that looks least rotten. First problem solved. The old man looks for a collar and a chain in the old shed. He even finds a dented dog food dish and an old coffee can for a water pail. Not that a water pail does much good in the winter, but I feel good that all is there and ready for Happy. I call her over and slip on her collar. I tie her to the chain while she licks my hand. The old man watches me.

"When I was a boy, we didn't have all them strays running around. The dogs were part of the family. In camp, they didn't need to be tied, just stuck around. In town, you keep them close.

They are your livelihood, your way to get around in the bush in winter."

"You are one lucky dog. You got two people looking out for you now," I say and pet Happy. "Good night, girl. I'll see you tomorrow."

I walk away. Happy follows me. When she reaches the end of her chain, she gets jerked back. Happy's yip is ear-piercing loud. Panicked, she runs in the opposite direction. The same thing happens, only worse, because this time she runs a lot faster.

"Happy, no!" I run to her and flop next to her in the snow. She cowers down and shakes like crazy. She doesn't dare to move. I stroke her gently until her shaking eases off a little.

"That dog has never been tied up. Just leave her alone—she'll get used it," the old man says.

I have to think of White Fang, and I can see the panicked trapped wild animal in Happy.

"Do we have to tie her up? Can't she be just loose like Acimosis?"

"She doesn't know that this is her home. If you want her to stay here, you tie her up."

"But she hates it!" I say.

"She is scared, because she don't understand why she can't run past the end of the chain. She get used to it. You come back tomorrow and see."

I pet her once more and then go away real quick, because I know if I look back one more time, I'd have to let her go. I'm just about at the road when I hear the old man call me back.

"One more thing: You find out who this dog belongs to. I don't want no trouble."

I nod, but I don't want to find out who Happy belongs to, because I already feel she belongs to me. What if someone wants her back?

11
CHAPTER

It's Monday morning, which means I have a whole week ahead of me before the next weekend. It's not that I mind school, but right now I really have more important things to do. I go to visit Happy before school and she does look a lot happier, but I can tell she's still awkward with her chain. She lifts up her feet and dances around the chain, trying not to touch it. It almost looks like she's scared it might snap at her. It would be really funny if she didn't look so sad.

At school, I draw a cartoon of Happy on my social studies paper. We are supposed to research how Canadian artists express a sense of place in their work. I don't even know what the teacher means by that. We're in the computer lab and I browse through a whole bunch of artwork pictures on Google Images. It's kind of boring, until I come upon this painting of a dog team.

There is something about it that catches my interest, although I can't really put my finger on it. The dogs and the sled look like the ones in the old photograph of the old man's dad. But that's not it. It's something about the land. It's so wide open and the dogs look tired, and so does the man, but they also look like they just belong there in that painting, in that landscape, in that cold.

It's an old painting and it's based on a photograph the painter took in 1953 on Lake Athabasca. It makes me kind of sad to think, if you go to Lake Athabasca now, the landscape is still there but the dog teams are not.

And then I find another picture that makes me even sadder. It's called "New Landscape," and there's this dog team sitting in the snow, and the musher has walked up to his dogs and they stare into the sunset. In front of the sun, there's this mine or oilrig, something big and industrial. Gray clouds of smoke are coming out of a big chimney and pollute the sky. The musher and the dogs just stand there, like there's no use for them anymore, no place to go.

I have to think of the old man and how he said there's no use for all his dog stuff anymore, and I feel like going over to him and telling him it's all wrong that there aren't any dog teams anymore, and that I do care, and that I want to listen to all his stories.

But I have to finish my social studies paper first. Then I have to learn how to build a fire.

Most importantly, I need to find out who Happy belongs to.

When I print out my social studies paper, I add one more page:

F O U N D !

Gray and white girl dog

Very happy. Likes Potato Chip bags. Looks like a sled dog.

If you are the owner or know the owner, phone Jeremy Cook.

Underneath, I put my phone number five times, so people can tear it off. I figure everyone in town has to buy groceries, gas, or check the mail. So I print one for Andy's (gas, mail, and the most important groceries, like milk, bread, and pop) and one for the North Mart (for everything else you can't buy at Andy's).

I hang up my poster right after school. Too late, I think about Poplar Point Trading Post. Some of the older people go there to buy groceries. So I scribble my message on the backside of a flyer I find on the street and hang it up there, too. I don't waste much time on the way home, because I want to get home before Mom does so I can take the calls.

★

MIRIAM KÖRNER

The first call I get is some little kids wondering if there's a reward. I tell them I found the dog. It's the LOST signs they have to look for, but I don't think they got it.

The second caller is a man.

"About that dog …" he says and I can feel my throat tighten.

"Yes?" I say.

"I got one just like that one. A Husky, eh? Only fifty bucks."

I sigh with relief, because he's not Happy's owner. I tell him I don't have any money right now.

"Forty. That's a good price. Ate more than that in dog food the year I had him."

"Maybe later," I say and hang up.

Then there are no more phone calls for quite a while. I just finished my homework when the phone rings. The third caller is a woman.

"Jeremy?" she asks. Her voice sounds familiar. "What's that dog business about? Where is it?"

Shoot, it's Mom!

"When I get home, I don't want that dog anywhere near my house. Or in my house."

"She's not here. She's with the old guy. He'll keep her for me." It's so silent, I can hear a car drive by from wherever Mom is phoning. Work, probably.

"We talk about that when I get home."

"Uhm … I … promised to help the old guy put in his net so I can feed Happy."

"You promised *me* not to go into the bush with the old guy! What happened to that?"

I can tell she wants to yell at me but she keeps her voice down, which means she's at work. The quiet yelling is worse.

"Look, Mom, it's not what you think," I say—although I'm not quite sure what she's thinking. "I'm not going into the bush. Just on the lake, right in front of town, okay?"

"What's the difference?! You step out of this town, you are in the bush. That's where we live, Jeremy. We are surrounded by wilderness, wherever you go!"

Now she's being unreasonable. "That's such baloney! Everyone and their dog hangs out on the lake. There's an ice road that goes halfway across the lake and people drive their trucks out there. It's not wilderness. It's a highway! I'm the only one in my class who isn't allowed to go skidooing with their buddies, and now I'm not even allowed to step a foot on the lake?! Come on, Mom."

"So what if there's a highway! People still sink their trucks and skidoos. People die out there, for crying out loud."

Last time I heard that someone drowned was two years ago, and he was really stupid. Went out with his truck near the river where most people don't even take their skidoos.

"They die on the highway going south, too! And if you look at the statistics, I bet more die in a car accident than an ice fishing accident!"

It's so silent on the other line that I hear three more cars drive by Mom's window before I realize what I just had said.

"I'm sorry, Mom, okay? I … I didn't mean to say that about the accident. It's just …"

"It's okay, Jeremy. You're right. I'm just worried about you, okay? And I don't like that you hang out with Jack."

"Mom, I'm thirteen. I can take care of myself, and he's just an old man."

"Let me finish, okay? There is something I want to tell you— maybe you'll understand. Meanwhile, just don't do anything stupid, okay? Never go so far that you can't see the town."

"Okay," I say, not because I agree, just so she can stop worrying. "What were you gonna tell me?"

"Not now, Jeremy."

"Mom, I told you, I'm thirteen. I'm not a little boy anymore."

"I know. Some other time, okay? Not on the phone."

There are no more callers about the dog after Mom's call. How long will I have to keep the sign up before I can say she's mine?

12
CHAPTER

I rummage through our freezer and find a freezer-burnt roast. I have no idea how long it takes to catch fish in a net, so I think brining the meat is a good idea.

The days are getting pretty short and it's already dark when I walk over to the old man's house. That's what I dislike about winter. It's dark when I walk to school and dark shortly after I get home. It even feels like there's less time during the day, as if the day doesn't have twenty-four hours anymore. I hadn't had a chance to build a fire yet. I tried out the flint and it was surprisingly easy to get some sparks going, but I never got enough of a flame to light the birch bark.

Happy is real happy to see me. She jumps at the end of her chain and, when I get within reach, she licks my hand like crazy. I let her loose and she runs around me in a circle. Acimosis chases Happy and grabs her by the neck. Happy flops into the deep snow and rolls over. Acimosis growls and chews on her neck.

"Acimosis! No!" I yell. I'm worried he'll hurt her, but then I realize it's just play. As soon as Acimosis lets off, Happy pushes against Acimosis until he grabs her by the neck again. It looks rough but he's real gentle.

Their play takes them toward the old shed. I notice light shining through the open door. The fishnet is lying on a tarp in the snow. A second later, the old man appears.

"I can't find my auger. Must have borrowed it to someone. This will do. That's all we had in the olden days." The old man passes me an ice chisel like the one I've seen by his waterhole. "Take that jigger, too." He nods toward a red board leaning against the shed. "Not too sure if we'll see it in the dark, but we'll give it a try. Your dog must be hungry."

"I got some meat," I say.

"That's good. There will be no fish today."

"What does Acimosis eat?"

"Same as me, but he can have fish now. Can't cook for all them dogs." His hand swoops over the general direction of the doghouses, and I get really excited when I picture a dog in each one of them.

"How many dogs do I need to have a team? Six?"

"For you, three or four will be good. Two was all my dad gave me when I was your age."

The old man puts the net into a tub and onto a little sled. I pick up the jigger. It's awkward to carry because of the levers that swing out. We walk down to the lake and then out on the ice of the bay and past the point. I look back. The lights of town are reflecting on the ice, and I can even make out the silhouette of the church tower in the bright moonlight. Good.

"Make a hole here." The old man draws an oval in the snow with his mukluk. It's about two feet long and a bit wider than the red board. Then he starts to roll out the net. I pick up the ice chisel, not quite sure what to do, and hit the ice. The tip of the chisel disappears in the snow. I can't really see what I'm doing, so I clear off the snow with my boots. I chip at the ice and little sharp pieces fly into my face. I'm not making much progress.

"Go around the edge. Like this." The old man takes the chisel and hits the ice. Big pieces break off and soon there's water seeping onto the ice. He hands the chisel back to me. "Put that string around your wrist. Don't want to lose that chisel. I've done that before, when I was a boy."

"Did you get it back?"

"I was lucky. We had the net in a couple days already. It was froze in a bit. Lost my chisel when I tried to chop it free. So my father cuts the ice with his axe and then we pull the net. There is a moray eel in the net and it's still alive. My father says, 'Now we get that chisel back.' I don't know what he means, so I just watch. He makes a little hole in the moray's jaw and ties blue fishing rope to it. Then he lets it go back through the hole.

The moray swims round and round in circles, winding the rope around the chisel. That's how my father could pull it up."

"Wow, really?" I'm not sure if he's pulling my leg but, if not, it's a neat story.

"No moray here now. So don't lose that chisel."

I chisel the ice around the edges like he has shown me. The center breaks off and I can take the ice out in one big piece. It's about six inches deep. That's a lot of ice for December. The lake has only been frozen for a couple of weeks.

"What did you used to do later in the year, when the ice is two feet thick?"

"Chisel a lot. Or not put a net in. If we can get enough in the fall, then we take the net out with first ice. Put it back in the spring when it's not going to freeze hard into the ice." The old man ties blue fishing rope to the jigger. Then he pushes the jigger under the ice. "You want to jig or listen where it goes?"

"Uhm … what's easier?"

"All depends on your ears. Mine don't hear very well anymore."

"Okay. What do I do?"

"Just follow the sound of the jigger."

The old man pulls on the rope and the red jigger starts moving under the ice with a metallic clicking sound. I've seen people set their nets in winter, but that was always from far away.

"That's so cool. How does it work?" I ask.

The old man explains how the jigger works, but I'm just getting more confused. There's a little arm with a sharp nail and, when you pull the rope, the arm moves forward and the nail gets stuck under the ice and pulls the board forward.

I guess some things you don't have to understand. You pull on the rope, the jigger moves, and that's it. All the jigger really is for is to pull the hundred or so feet of blue fishing rope under the ice, so you can pull the net through. I get that.

"Are you following the sound?"

"Mhm?"

"The clicking, you hear that?"

"Yes," I say, but it's kind of hard to follow the sound if you can't see where it comes from. I put my head closer to the ice and try to catch up to the clicking. After about a hundred feet of walking, the clicking stops.

"Is it there?" The old man asks.

"I think so."

The old man pulls on the line. Click.

"Right under your feet?"

I move over two feet. "Ahm ... I think it's here."

Click. I step back another foot. "It's here. I think."

"Move the snow and have a look."

I scrape the snow with my boot until I can see clear ice. At first that's all I see, just the ice, but when I hear the clicking again, I see something move under the ice.

"It's here. I found it! I found it!" I kneel down and scrape the ice clear with my mitts. "Right here! What next?"

I'm so excited I could do a jig of my own on the ice, but then I feel stupid about it. The old man must have done this a million times. For him, it's probably just work, like doing dishes or something boring like that.

"Neat, eh?" The old man passes me the ice chisel and smiles at me. "That jigger works pretty good. When I was a boy, we used to push a long pole under the ice, make a hole where it ends and push it out some more, and then do it all over again until we can pull the net through. This here is a lot easier."

I think about the power auger Justin and I used when we went fishing with his dad, while I chisel another hole to pull the jigger out. The water is cold, and I quickly dry my hands off on my pants as soon as I got the jigger onto the ice. The old man unties the rope and hands it to me, then walks over to the net.

"Pull, now!" He calls and guides the net under the ice. When the net is tied to the blocks of ice I chiseled, the old man covers the holes with snow.

"Tomorrow we'll have some fish. Now, let's build a fire to warm up."

"I … uhm …" I say. I still don't know how to make a fire with my flint.

"See that birch tree over there? That's got good bark. Skinny like paper."

We walk over to the point. I tear the bark off and the old man clears the snow off the ground. He breaks off a couple big branches from a dead tree and lays them over the exposed moss. On top, he places lichen and little twigs, then bigger sticks.

"Put your bark right here."

I stuff it under the green lichen and the old man passes me his matches. One strike and the fire eats its way hungrily through the bark and lichen, and then the flames jump onto the sticks. We add bigger and bigger sticks until we have a nice fire. Not huge, but big enough to warm our hands. The flames light up the old man's face.

"Tomorrow we have fish."

His eyes look shiny like a little boy's the night before Christmas.

CHAPTER 13

I can't believe it's Saturday. This week went by so fast. I learned so many new things, and they're already part of my day-to-day life.

Building a fire with my flint isn't a big deal anymore, since I figured out how to use really, really skinny pieces of birch bark and make a tiny, tiny bowl with them to catch the sparks. And then I just have to add fine strings of old man's beard. That's that lichen that hangs from the branches of the swampy spruce trees behind the old man's house.

I fixed up three more doghouses with an old signboard I found at the dump. I put a second house in Happy's circle, because Acimosis likes to steal Happy's house and she was sleeping in a snow bank. Now they sleep next to each other, each in their own house.

One afternoon, we repaired the old toboggan, and I learned how to use an awl to fix some of the stitching that came loose on the old harnesses.

We also gave the dogs some tobacco. To get rid of worms. That's what they used to do because, back then, you couldn't go to the drug store and buy pills for your dogs.

We check the net every day and we pull out so much fish, we could feed a whole dog team. The old man keeps the pickerel cheeks and fillets, and the dogs get a soup of the heads and guts, suckers, and whitefish. We feed some right away and freeze some in chunks to feed later. We even have extra fish to give to the Elders at the old folks apartments.

★

Today, the net is really heavy! No wonder. There are eighteen fish in the net. My fingers start to hurt after untangling the third one, and it's not even that cold today. The faster I try to work, the more the fish seem to get tangled. The old man works slowly, as if the cold doesn't bother him.

"That's a good catch, eh?" I ask, trying to cheer myself up.

"Good catch now maybe, but not in the olden days. You couldn't leave the net in for two days. Too many fish. Lots of people fished on Poplar Lake back then. They drove out there with cat trains, fishing all the time."

"For the dogs?"

"No, no. Commercially. They processed it in the fish plant and then shipped it down south."

"Fish plant? Here? Is it still there?"

"You know that blue building next to where the Hudson Bay post used to be? That's the old plant."

I think I know the building, although I don't know where the Hudson Bay post was. I didn't know we had a fish plant. If it's the building I'm thinking of, then it's all boarded up now. It's kind of cool that he still remembers it. I bet there aren't many people left who actually lived that part of history—I mean, trading fur and fish for flour and sugar and all that. And having a dog team for transportation.

★

Nobody's claimed Happy yet and I worry less and less that someone will. It feels more and more like she's my dog now. I'm getting to know her better and better. She comes when I call her, but that was easy to teach because she always wants to come.

It's a lot harder to make her stay, but the old man won't let me put a harness on her until she knows "stay." So after warming up from dealing with the fish, I try again to teach her.

It's hard, because I don't know how to train dogs. I tell her, "Stay," and kind of wait to see what happens. Nothing happens. Happy totally ignores it. We try over and over, but nothing works.

The old man is watching me but he doesn't say a thing. I start to doubt that Happy will ever learn.

"What shall I do?"

"The dog, she can tell you don't believe she's gonna listen."

"She does?"

"Try again. This time believe she will stay."

"Stay!" I say to Happy. Please stay, I think. But it doesn't make a difference. She's running around me as if she wants to play a game of tag.

The old man draws a line in the snow.

"Past this line here is unsafe ice. If your dog crosses that line, she break through." He grabs Happy by the collar and drags her across the line. "Stay," he says.

There's no question mark attached to his command and Happy hunkers down. When he walks away, Happy wants to run to me, but I'm right there by the line.

"No! Stay." I have the picture in my head of Happy drowning if I can't make her stay. I hold my hands up to show her I wouldn't let her cross the line. And it makes a difference!

Happy shifts from one paw to the other but she doesn't cross the line.

MIRIAM KÖRNER

"Down," I say, and this time all my focus is on Happy. I imagine how I might push her down with my hand like I did before but, this time, I do it with my voice only. And Happy lies down!

It seems like she suddenly understands that when I talk to her, I want her to do a certain thing, and she's getting better at figuring out what I want.

We practice "sit," "down," "stay," and "come." Acimosis runs along and sometimes he listens to the commands I give to Happy, but only if he knows I have treats in my pockets for rewards.

Things are going real good, but then Happy slinks away. She has had enough. Like a kid in school at the end of the day. I call her one more time and tell her what a good dog she is. I pet her and then I let her run off with Acimosis.

I watch them play and I picture myself in a yard full of dogs, all wagging their tails as soon as they see me. I go around and pet every one, and then I harness them and hook them up to my toboggan. I tell them, "Down," and they all wait patiently until I step on the running board. As soon as I say, "Let's go," we rush out of the yard and onto the lake, and I feel the cool breeze in my face.

There's only one problem with this picture: I only have one dog—maybe two, but I'm not sure if the old man will let me use Acimosis. Sometimes I feel as if it's all just pretend play. When I was little, my cousin and I used to pretend our stuffies were sled dogs. We tied them to a shoebox and mushed them on the living room carpet, but I would never tell this to anyone now.

14
CHAPTER

Justin calls me the Dogless Dog Whisperer, and that's not even the worst thing he said since our fight. It hurts and gives me a reason to show him the cold shoulder, but I think it's a bit of a cop-out on my part. It's easier to be mad at Justin than to tell him I don't have time for him, and I don't want him to meet Happy and the old man. Partly because I'm worried he'll do something hurtful to my dog, partly because I don't feel like sharing the whole thing with Justin. I'm scared he thinks it's ridiculous, and then I might find it ridiculous, too.

★

I really wish I had more dogs. Yesterday, I put up a new poster in town.

DOG WANTED!

Young, strong dog, preferably Husky or Husky mix

Will provide a good home

So far, nobody called.

Finding Happy was so easy. I wasn't even looking for a dog then. It's more like she came to me. So I thought it would be easy to find a couple more dogs. There are so many roaming the streets but they don't look like they could pull a sled.

After my chores, I walk down the streets looking for dogs. I meet two on our street who have a body about Happy's size, but their legs are only half as long. On Maskwa Drive, there's a whole pack of dogs. Two are puppies and I don't know what they'll be when they grow up. They follow a brown dog around, who can barely see through the long hair in her face. And then there's a German Shepherd-looking one. He snaps at the puppies and I make a detour around him to stay well clear.

There's another one in that pack. He's black and white. One ear is standing up, the other one flopping down. He looks the most sled-doggish. He's a bit taller than Happy and a bit smaller than Acimosis. His legs seem to fit the rest of his body.

He's friendly and I pet him for a while. I wonder if he would make a good sled dog and if I should just take him and try him out. But I don't know if this is right. I don't want anybody thinking I'm a dog thief. Plus, the dog looks quite happy, hanging out with his buddies. He might not even want to come with me. I sigh. Maybe this whole dog team business is a stupid idea after all. Better to go home.

I count three more dogs on my way, but only one looks anything like a sled dog. I've seen him many times before. He's always tied up to a big black garbage container. When the container is full, he just lies there like he's guarding his treasure chest. When it's empty, he sometimes drags it behind him. It's real heavy and he can never move it more than a couple feet. He's kind of shy and ducks away when I try to pet him, and then he walks right close to me when I walk away. It's like he doesn't really know what he wants. He's curious but scared. He's gray and white with bits of brown. I call him Saddric. 'Cause he could be Happy's brother, except he's more sad than happy.

"Hey, Saddric, how are you today?" I hold out my hand and Saddric sniffs it. He stands as far back from me as he can and then leans forward. I always expect him to fall over but he never does. Today he even lets me pet his chin. I like him. He seems gentle and thoughtful.

"You should have bought that dog when I only wanted fifty bucks for it. Now he cost a hundred."

I recognize the voice immediately. It's the same man who phoned me last week. His voice is kind of throaty like some of the country singers on MBC radio. But not unfriendly. I turn and look at a man about my mom's age. I'm not sure if he's just messing with me, so I say nothing.

"You wanna know why?"

"Hmm?"

"'Cause I dropped my watch in the driveway and he ate it. That watch was fifty bucks." He laughs and I force myself to smile.

"No, serious. You want that dog? Fifty bucks." He holds out his hand as if about to close the deal.

"I don't have any money." I turn to leave, but then I have an idea. "I could bring you fish."

"If you can't buy him, I can lease him to you. He's yours to keep, but if you win any races with him, then I get my cut. That's what they do on the Iditarod, you know. If you cross the finish line with ten dogs and Cheerio here is in your team, I get a tenth of your winning. If you win that big fancy truck, it's at least four tires for me and then some." He slaps my shoulder. "What do you think, Lance?"

"Jeremy," I say.

"Jeremy Cook, Lance Mackey, all the same. Don't tell me you never heard of the Iditarod?"

Sure, I had. Who hasn't heard of the longest and toughest sled dog race on earth? And Mackey is the coolest musher. He's had a real hard upbringing and not much money, and cancer and stuff, and he still won it a few times—but that's not the point.

"I'm not racing dogs," I say.

"You're not? What you got sled dogs for, then?"

"How do you know I got sled dogs?"

"Small town. Everyone knows the Cooks are getting back into dogs."

The Cooks? Yeah, right, like my mom would want to be involved.

"I only got one so far," I mumble.

"Two, now." He ties a piece of rope to Cheerio/Saddric's collar and hands me the makeshift leash.

★

By the time I arrive with Cheerio at his new home, my hand is just about bleeding from the rope tied to it. He was right at the end of the rope the whole way, pulling sideways to be as far away from me as he possibly could. He's so strong! No doubt, he'll be a good sled dog. Pulled me along as if I wasn't even there. All I could do is get him going in the right direction and then hang on. I hope nobody from school saw how he was taking me for a walk.

Now that he's with Happy and Acimosis, he's totally changed. He doesn't play as rough as Acimosis and he isn't bouncy like Happy, but he's a lot more relaxed now. He's like the little kid that stands at the edge of the playground and wants to play with the big kids but doesn't know what to say. When they let him play with them, he's still kind of shy, but he can't hide his happiness.

Cheerio's panting with his mouth open. His tongue hangs out and I'm not sure if he's nervous or hot, but he looks like he's got a big smile on his face. There's no fight with the chain when I tie him up. He can still reach Happy when they're both at the end of their chains. And that's where he sits, tight and close to her. Like he always belonged there. Maybe my dream about a dog team wasn't so stupid after all. Maybe Justin will stop calling me the Dogless Dog Whisperer now that I'm getting my own team. I whistle while I walk around the dog yard and shovel pooh into a bucket.

★

The old man comes out to inspect my new dog.

"This is …" I don't know what to say now. "His real name is Cheerio, but to me he's a Saddric. What should I call him? Maybe it's best not to confuse him with a new name."

"In the olden days, a dog had to earn his name, you know. We never named our dogs until they had proven themselves. If it was a real good dog, he got a name like TwoDog or Fast Runner. Others were just called Blackie or Narrow Tail."

"What about Acimosis? Where did he get his name?"

"Acimosis proved himself when he was a puppy."

"What did he do?"

The old man strokes Acimosis's head. "You saved a boy's life, didn't you?"

Acimosis puts his paw onto the old man's arm and whines quietly as if he's talking. I want to know in the worst way how he saved a boy's life, but I know it's not the moment to ask. It's like there's no room for me in the silent conversation he's having with his dog. So I just chop up some frozen fish, get water from the ice hole, and build a fire to boil the fish soup. I've built a fire so many times now that I don't even have to think anymore. Although I don't use my flint very often. Matches are a lot faster.

★

"So that's the famous dog team."

I whirl around when I hear Justin's voice. The fish soup boils over and it starts to reek of burnt fish. I quickly grab the pot and set it in the snow.

"How did you know I was here?" I ask.

"Let's see. A raven told me? Clever detective work? Or was it your mom?" Justin sweeps his hand through the air like a wizard about to crush his enemy's empire. "You could have told me, you know."

"Told you what?"

"About the dogs."

"I didn't think you were interested."

"Says who?" Justin's voice is sharp. His eyes are glaring.

I hear a low growl behind me and turn around.

The old man is chopping wood. Acimosis is standing in front of him. His head is lowered; his ears are back and his hair standing up. He is staring at Justin. This is not good. I have to get Justin out of here. Fast. But how?

"I did tell you I was wanting to train a dog team," I say.

"I thought you were totally nuts, and I guess I'm right. So this is it, then? That's how you spend your weekends? Come on, let's do something fun. This place is depressing."

"You go ahead. I ... I still have to feed the dogs." It sounds more like a question, like I need Justin to be okay with it. He's not.

"What happened to you? We used to hang out, play videogames, own the street—and now what? You shovel shit for fun? Remember we came here and you pulled that dog's tail? That was fun. Just you and me."

I glance over to the old man and hope he doesn't hear what Justin is yelling.

"Okay, okay," I say.

"No. Not okay!"

Suddenly I'm scared of Justin—or for Justin. I don't know which. I just wish he wouldn't yell at me. Acimosis walks toward us. His growl is deep and guttural. Justin must hear it, too.

"I think you should go," I say to Justin, because I'm worried about what might happen when Acimosis gets here.

"What? Is that what you want? Fine. Your choice. Don't come begging to me when you're bored with all this."

He gets up and I want to call, "Wait," and explain everything to him, but he's already past Cheerio's circle. Happy runs, tail wagging, toward Justin, and that's when he kicks her. Happy yips and runs into her house. Acimosis leaps toward Justin.

"Acimosis!" The old man's voice sounds like a whiplash. Acimosis sits down, but his hair is still up, his eyes following Justin as he makes his way down the road.

"Don't ever come back here," I yell after him. When I sit down with Happy, I realize I'm not mad. Just sad.

"Your friend?" The old man is suddenly behind me.

I shrug. "Not really."

"I feed the dogs. You catch up with your friend."

"Thanks," I say.

I walk down the road but, when I come to the junction, I don't follow Justin. I go home and crawl into bed, even though it's not even dark yet.

15
CHAPTER

It's warm and dark and cozy where I am; kind of like under my blankets. I can feel something wet pressing against my cheek. I can hear a muffled voice talking quietly. It sounds far off, like when you're not quite awake.

"Good dogs," the voice says. It sounds familiar, but I don't know who it belongs to. There are other sounds, too. Like something heavy being dragged through the snow and the quiet panting of dogs. Haha, ha, hahaha. It sounds melodic, like a drumbeat, and I get sleepy, real sleepy.

"Jeremy," a voice calls. This one I've heard before.

★

Suddenly it's light all around me.

"Are you sick? How come you're in bed at five in the afternoon? On a Saturday, of all days?" Mom is holding my blankets in her arm. She looks concerned.

"I'm fine," I mumble. I try to go back to my dream but it's too late. I'm wide awake.

"Did you feed your dog?"

"Hmm."

Mom has been real good about letting me keep Happy at the old man's place. I'm kind of worried to break the news to her.

"I got two now. You know Lynx Road? That dog that's always tied to the garbage bin? The owner didn't want him. Do you know the guy? He said something strange. Like the Cooks had dogs before or something?" I say it all real quick, like it's just some small-talk, like a "How's school?" kind of deal. Mom nods and sits down.

"I think I know who you mean. He's always wearing a red lumberjack jacket and he's always joking?"

"Yeah, that's him."

"You watch him! He'd sell you a dog even though it wasn't his own." Mom smiles and I know she's just kidding. Then her face turns serious.

"Your dad's family had dogs. They were the last ones here who still had working dogs. There are other Cooks, though, but they're way up in Caribou Narrows. They have racing dogs. Maybe he just got the Cooks mixed up."

"Did my dad have dogs?"

"No, he never had his own dogs. He … oh, oh, the potatoes!" I can hear water splashing onto the hot stove, and Mom runs out of my room to save supper.

CHAPTER 16

I can't believe how many people want to get rid of their dogs—or their neighbor's dog, because there were quite a few kids who tried to sell me their dog, and I'm sure it wasn't theirs. I had several calls today and Mom told me someone phoned yesterday, as well. That's probably why she wasn't surprised when I told her about my new dog. We agreed on no more than three dogs, which is the town limit, she said. With Acimosis, we'd be one over the limit, but I don't bother her with my math skills.

Plus, I don't think anybody cares how many dogs I have except Mom. I promised her she won't have to remind me to go

MIRIAM KÖRNER

feed them. She still doesn't trust the old man, but I think she's okay with what I'm doing now.

So I'm looking for one more dog. I should have been more precise with my description on my poster—put on a minimum height or something. Even when I tell people I want a dog that can pull a sled, they still try to give me their shorties. One guy told me they used to have fun races in town a long time ago. Only dogs under a foot were allowed. Fine, but I don't want his miniature poodle. I keep thinking of that black and white dog with the floppy ear, but his owner doesn't call.

I look at a lot of dogs before I find one I like. He's just about all black. His feet are light brown and he has a dot above each of his eyes. There's a bit of light brown on the side of his face. It looks like a lightning strike. The owner gives him a nudge with his boot as a goodbye present. His kids had wanted a puppy but had grown bored with him, and now he's just a nuisance, the owner tells me.

"So don't bring him back," he says and closes the door. I bend down and whisper in the dog's ear that he'll never be a nuisance to me and not to worry: I won't bring him back. After that, he just follows me like he always belonged to me. It's kind of strange. It feels like I've known him forever, even though I've never seen him before. We're already past the gravel pile in that muskegy area where they're trying to build new houses, before I realize I never asked for the dog's name. I want to call him Lightning because of his markings, but then I decide to wait till I run him. Then I can give him the name he deserves.

★

I think the old man likes my new dog. When he sees me coming into the yard with Lightning following me, he nods, kind of pleased, and brings the harnesses out from the shed.

"Try this one."

It slips easily over Lightning's head.

"No good. Too loose."

He passes me another one and I have to really wiggle it to get it over his head.

"Good."

I try on harnesses until I have one for each dog. Happy, Cheerio, and Lightning. I turn to tell the old man that I'm ready, but then I say nothing. He's bent down with one knee in the snow and his arm leaning on his other knee. Acimosis is wearing a harness and they have one of their quiet conversations. I feel my stomach turn all warm and fuzzy inside. Acimosis is in my team! But then the old man takes the harness off again. And everyone else's as well.

"Remember now what harness goes on what dog. We mark them and then they are all ready for you next week."

"Next week? Why can't I go now?"

"Dogs are too new. Don't know you yet. It's okay if you only have one new dog in the team, but all new dogs is no good."

I follow him inside and write the dogs' names on the leather straps of each harness. I leave Lightning's blank.

"You got to know your dogs. That's the difference between a good dog driver and not so good dog driver. You need to find the right language."

"What language do you mean? Cree or English?"

The old man laughs. "Sometimes that, too. In our family, we always used '*u*' and '*cha*' for dogs. One day I get this new dog. Supposed to be a real good leader. Goes across the lake with no track to follow. So I try him out. Each time I want to turn right, I call '*cha*,' when I go left, I call '*u*.' The new dog just looks at me and keeps going straight. I try and try but he's no good. So I put him back in the team. I'm upset because I paid a lot of money for this dog.

"Then there's the winter festival race. Tom keeps poking fun of me because I don't want to race. So finally I enter. Tom's team is right close by me when we come to the turn-around loop. Tom calls 'haw' and the new dog jumps left like a bullet hit him. Pulls the leaders over and we make such a tight circle that we pass Tom on the inside and win the race. I laughed and laughed and laughed. My dog speaks only English!"

The old man smiles. He's grabbing onto the backrest of his chair like he's holding the handlebar of his toboggan.

"What did you do then? Use gee and haw instead?"

"Only for a short while. Once I knew what the dog knew, it wasn't hard to teach him *u* and *cha*."

"What should I use for my dogs?"

"It doesn't matter what language you speak, as long as you talk dog."

★

It's not until Saturday the following week that we finally hook the dogs up to the sled. My heart is beating super-fast. I can't wait to get going.

Only problem is: the dogs are not going anywhere. I put Acimosis in lead, because I know him the longest, then Happy, Cheerio, and Lightning. The way the dogs are hooked up is the old style. Single file, the old man calls it. One dog behind the other with traces on both sides. My team looks real long this way. Like an eight-dog team if you hook them up tandem like the racers do.

"Let's go! Hike! Mush!" Happy turns over in her harness and gets tangled in her traces. She tries to play with Cheerio behind her, but she can't reach, so she starts chewing on the traces. The old man grabs her nose and shakes it before she can chew through the leather. Acimosis looks at the old man and wags his tail. Looks like he's waiting for us to go for a walk with him. Cheerio pulls sideways to get as far away as possible from the old man standing next to the team. Lightning is the only one who is rocking back and forth like he's trying to get the sled moving.

"What do I do?" I ask.

"Look at your dogs. They are telling you what to do."

"They are?"

"Put the one in lead who looks like a leader, the one who wants to go."

I switch Lightning for Acimosis, which is kind of hard to do, because Lightning is in the very back, and I have to unhook everyone to change their positions. I can't hold on to all the dogs at once and Cheerio takes off for his house. By the time I coax him back out again, the rest of the dogs have pulled the hook loose and dragged the sled over to the shed where we keep the frozen fish.

I look for the old man for help. He stands next to his cabin, smiling from ear to ear. He's enjoying the show. I'm mad for a second that he doesn't help me, but then I think probably I would find it funny as well if it was someone else. It's just not funny if it's you who's being laughed at.

"Hey! Enough of this. You all know 'down.' And I mean it. Down!" I drag the dogs to the positions they're supposed to be in and make them stay. I really, really try hard to believe they will stay, but I'm still surprised when they actually do.

I pull my snow hook. "Let's go!"

When Lightning takes off, the rest of the dogs follow. We fly out of the yard just like I pictured it. For about a hundred meters. Then Happy starts bouncing and looking back. A second later, she's being dragged through the snow. The team stops. Happy rolls happily in the snow and tries to lick Cheerio's face. She's so tangled that I can't figure out how to straighten out the traces.

So I unclip everyone again. Happy and Cheerio take off back home. Acimosis looks at me and then he looks at Happy and Cheerio running flat out down the trail. It doesn't take him long to decide where he wants to be. In a blink, he's gone, too. I'm left with Lightning. I'm a bit mad with the dogs for just leaving me here. Lightning stands next to me and whines.

"Thanks for staying, Buddy." I pet Lightning behind his ears and he stops whimpering. "I guess it's just you and me to bring the sled back."

I pick up the traces and pull. I'm surprised how heavy the sled is. When the dogs pulled it, it seemed there was nothing to it. The toboggan slid and skidded across the snow so fast that I was relieved when the dogs stopped. I wasn't sure if I could keep it upright much longer. Now I wish they were here.

"Acimosis, Happy, Cheerio!" I have to call three times before they come blasting down the trail. Their mouths are open and their tongues are flopping and their tails flailing. They look so happy, I can't even be mad with them anymore. Happy and Acimosis pile on top of me and lick my face. I fall over laughing. Cheerio runs around us in a circle just out of my reach, and Lightning barks at the whole scene.

"Hey!" I say. "You're supposed to be sled dogs! Come on, let's try again."

I scramble to my feet and clip Happy to the sled. I can't catch Cheerio, so I clip Acimosis in next. Lightning walks to the front of the team like that's where he wants to be. He looks like a sprint racer waiting for the countdown.

"Okay!" I call, and Lightning leaps forward. The other two dogs follow and Cheerio runs next to Happy. We're back at the yard in no time at all. Happy doesn't turn around once, and I think it's because there's no dog behind her to play with, so she tries catching up with the dog in front instead and pulls real hard. I take the harnesses off and tie the dogs back to their houses. I have to drag Cheerio out of Happy's house, because as soon as I tie up Happy, he goes into her house, harness and lines and all.

"I see you are back," the old man smiles at me. "What did you learn?"

"That dog sledding isn't easy?" I ask.

"Tell me what you learned about your dogs."

"Mhm ... that Lightning makes a good leader?"

"What makes you think so?"

"I don't know. It's almost like he's always trying to figure out what I want. And then when he gets it right, it makes him real happy. Like he would do anything for me if he only understood what I'm telling him. Not like Happy. She just comes along for the fun of it, but she doesn't really care if we're running or playing, or whatever, as long as she's happy. I mean, it's not like she doesn't care about me. I think it makes her happy when I'm happy, but I don't think she spends too much time figuring out what I want. I ... I don't know. Does that make sense?"

"Very much. What about the others?"

"I think Cheerio might be all right. He's just so scared. It's like he'd rather not try because he doesn't want to make a mistake or get hurt. Like he's got no confidence. If he would only trust me, I think he would be a good sled dog."

The old man nods and I can tell he's pleased with what I tell him.

"What about Acimosis?"

"Acimosis? I don't know. That's the strange thing. I thought I knew him the best, but I don't really know now. When Happy and Cheerio took off, he looked at me first and I thought he would stay with me, but he didn't."

"Did you tell him?"

"What?"

"Did you tell him to stay?"

"No, I never even thought of it."

The old man nods again and walks to the house, and I realize that my first lesson wasn't about running the dogs, but about getting to know them.

CHAPTER 17

It's barely daylight when I hook up my four dogs on Sunday. This time there's no question about the order. Happy is in wheel—that's what the old man calls the position closest to the sled.

"The wheel dog is your steering," he said. "That dog helps the sled turn." I don't know if Happy is a good wheel dog. I just put her there so nobody is behind her. That way she won't get so distracted. In front of her is Cheerio and then Acimosis, and Lightning is in lead.

The dogs are just as excited as I am. Happy barks non-stop; Cheerio pants and drools; Acimosis jumps like crazy; and Lightning rocks back and forth, trying to get the sled moving. I bend down to pull my hook, when the old man steps on it.

"This is not good. They are not ready to go."

"Not ready? Looks to me like they can't wait!"

"That's right. They can't wait. So they better learn to wait. I put the kettle on."

Am I supposed to follow him or stay with the dogs until he's back? I walk up to the dogs and tell them to stay. Each one listens when I talk to them. The only problem: they don't listen all at the same time. As soon as I turn my attention from Happy to Cheerio, Happy is up on her feet and barking again. The only one who settles down is Acimosis. Cheerio cowers down as soon as I look at him but he, too, doesn't stay for long. I glance toward the cabin. The old man watches me from the open door. He holds a teacup in each hand and raises one to me.

"Stay!" I say one more time. This time I really mean it, because I don't want them ending up at the fish pile again.

"Thanks," I say and take my teacup, even though I don't really feel like drinking tea. The tea burns my mouth, so I add some snow to make it cool off faster. I turn around, expecting my team to be in total disorder and am surprised to see them patiently sitting in the snow, looking at me. It's almost like they're part of our tea party and totally relaxed. It's cool to see that the dogs understand me better and better. And so quick, too.

Even cooler to figure out that each one of them behaves so differently. As if they all have a different personality.

Acimosis's head is resting on his front paws and he's almost falling asleep. I can tell Lightning is still ready to go, but he's less tense. As if he's saying, "Whenever you're ready." Happy is licking the fur on her belly, like cleaning is the only thing she's got on her mind. Cheerio sits so motionless, I have to look real closely to see that he's even breathing.

"Can I go now?" I ask.

"The dogs are ready. Are you?"

That's when I get that my second lesson is about patience. I finish my tea and even clean the mug. Then I walk over to the dogs. As soon as I step on the back of the toboggan, the dogs jump up.

"No! Down!" I command as I walk up to them. This time all four settle down. When I get back onto the sled, only Happy jumps up and starts barking. Acimosis's bum is about two inches off the snow, between sitting and standing.

"Down!" Happy and Acimosis sit.

Four more times I have to remind them, but then everyone is waiting patiently. I pull the hook.

"Let's go!" I say.

Lightning looks at me and stands up slowly. "You mean go now?" he seems to ask.

Acimosis's bum lifts off the snow.

"Good dogs!" When they hear my praise, they happily take off down the trail and out onto the lake.

The dogs follow the trail to the waterhole and then past the spot where we had the net until yesterday. It's too cold now to leave it in and, besides, we got quite a few tubs of fish for the dogs. When the dogs reach the end of our trail, Lightning stops so suddenly that Acimosis runs over him.

"Keep going!" I call.

Lightning is standing in snow up to his chest and looks at me.

"You don't know where to go? Just go straight."

Lightning wags his tail and runs toward me.

"No!" I call and throw my hook in. I run up to Lightning and straighten the team out. Happy is hopelessly tangled. Instead of undoing her lines, I roll her over and over until she's sorted out again. I'm getting sweaty, even though it's a cold day.

Everything went so well until we came to the end of the trail on the lake. Why doesn't Lightning want to go any further? At least we came twice as far as last time. I think about turning around to go home, but then I get an idea. Maybe they need a trail to follow. Or at least understand which direction I want them to go.

I walk ahead of the team. It's like I'm the lead dog now. The dogs want to follow me in the worst way.

"STAY!" I yell, but everyone is bouncing and pulling and barking. I'm worried they'll take off without me, so I only walk a couple of dog team lengths and run back to my toboggan as fast as I can.

"Okay!" The dogs follow my tracks. When they reach the end where I walked, Lightning only hesitates for a second.

"Keep going. Atta good boy!"

There's a skidoo trail ahead of us. Lightning sees it, too. He runs straight for the trail and makes a sharp ninety-degree corner when he reaches the skidoo track. The dogs pick up speed when they hit the hard-packed trail. The sled whips around the corner. Next thing I know, I'm face down in the snow. The sled is tipped on its side.

"Whoa!" I yell, but the dogs have stopped already. I crawl through the snow and, when I find my footing, I lift up the sled. Before I'm back on the runners, the dogs take off. I'm pulled off my feet and the next thing I know I'm dragging behind.

"Whoa!" I yell, but this time no one listens. I lose the grip on the sled with my left hand and my right arm feels like it's being pulled out of its socket. I want to let go, but I remember the old man telling me never to let go of your dog team. In fact, that's pretty much all he ever told me about the how-to of running dogs. So I hang on.

"Whoa!" I yell again. But they don't stop until the toboggan hits a snowdrift and the sled tips over.

Now there's enough drag that the dogs stop. I carefully grab my hook and put it into the snow before I lift up the sled. Phew … the hook is holding and I crawl back onto my feet.

I tell the dogs, "Down," and pause for a while to catch my breath and gather the courage to pull the hook. I didn't think four dogs could have so much power. It's kind of scary, because I'm not sure who's in control: the dogs or me. But it's also lots of fun. In fact, I can't remember the last time when I had so much fun. Maybe when we went tobogganing in the gravel pit.

★

I was eight, Justin nine. We were still doing kid stuff then, nothing of that awkwardness and not knowing what to say, like now.

We borrowed a skidoo toboggan, which really isn't so different from my dog sled. Same kind of boards with the curl in the front, except wider and heavier. There were ten of us and we dragged it the whole two miles to the gravel pit. Some of us pulling, the other ones riding. Once on top of the gravel pile, we all climbed into the sled. We got going real fast and then we hit that big rock. The sled stopped dead in its tracks and we all flew out, one after the other, and landed on top of each other. We laughed so hard, that Leon peed his pants, and then we laughed even more.

Funny that I'm thinking of it now because, back then, I imagined the kids pulling the sled were my dogs and I was a musher.

I wish Justin could see me now.

"Let's go." The dogs run down the skidoo trail toward the islands in the distance. I carefully turn to look back. I can still see smoke from the houses, but the town is harder and harder to make out from the surrounding shoreline.

Time to head back. I don't know the command for turn around, or if there is even such a thing, so when I see a skidoo track cross ours, I call, "Haw!"

The dogs keep going straight. I try the Cree version. "*U!*"

Lightning turns his head, but keeps going straight.

"*U!*" I try again.

Lightning stops.

"No! *U!*"

Lightning starts running again. He looks back while he's running. It's almost like he's got a big question mark written in his face. I guess my dogs speak neither English nor Cree.

"Turn left!" I try one more time.

It's like trying to get a two-year-old to bring you a can of pop from the fridge. First they offer you their LEGO, then they point at their teddy, and when you finally get them to open the fridge, they bring you the mustard. I think Lightning would turn left if only he knew what I wanted. How can I make him understand?

"Whoa!" I scrape my hook through the snow and, when the dogs feel its resistance, they stop. "Look! *U!*" I say and stomp a circle in front of Lightning that turns back to the skidoo track we came on.

Lightning wags his tail and follows the trail I stomped. I pull my hook and we take off toward the dog yard.

"That's it! That's what *u* means." I'm so proud of my dogs that I can't stop smiling. When we round the point by the cabin, I can make out a figure on the ice. First I think it's the old man coming to see where I am, but when I get closer, I can tell he's much younger. It's Justin!

"Hey, Justin! Look at this!" I call and wave at him wildly.

Then I remember we're not exactly friends anymore. I'm glad he's too far away to hear me. I hope he didn't see me wave so stupidly.

The figure disappears between the trees, and I'm not sure anymore if it even was Justin. What would he have been doing behind the old man's cabin?

★

When I go to feed the dogs on Monday, I notice snowshoes leaning against the shed. The old man tells me to snowshoe loops onto the lake, so I can teach my dogs left and right. It's late by the time I'm done, and I have to wait till the next day to try out my trails.

On Tuesday, I take out Lightning and Acimosis. Just the two of them, so I have more control. Every time we come to a crossroads, I tell them *u* or *cha*. First I have to run ahead of them to show them. But it doesn't take long and they're turning on their own.

I'm wiped out and sweaty when I get back, but I think both understand that *u* and *cha* means to turn. They still haven't figured out which is which. They just try one way, and when I say, "No," they try the other direction. To make matters worse: I got mixed up a couple times myself, so when I'm home, I write *u* for left and *cha* for right on my big mitts. I'm amazed how much progress we made and how easy everything has been so far. Almost too easy.

CHAPTER 18

I'm in a real good mood Wednesday morning, even though I'm stuck at school and we have a math test in third period. Justin was late, so there isn't any awkward ignoring and glaring at each other. I don't care anyway, because after school I'll take my dogs for a run. I can't wait to see if Lightning will listen to "left" and "right" even with the whole team behind him. I picture myself being pulled down the trail, I call "*cha*," and then …

BANG!

A distant rifle shot pulls me out of my daydream. Then there's another shot. This one sounds closer. I hear a heartbreaking squeal, another shot, and then silence. You could hear a safety pin hit the floor, it's so quiet in our classroom. Even the teacher stops talking mid-sentence.

I bite my lip real hard, trying to stop the tears from welling up. I heard it on the radio yesterday. Some kid got chased by a pack of dogs last week and got bitten pretty bad. The parents were really upset and now it's here. Dog-shooting day.

I double-checked all the chains and snaps last night, but I still have a real sick feeling in my stomach. I want to be with my dogs. But I can't just walk out and miss the math test. That's when Annika passes me the note. I recognize Justin's handwriting right away.

Remember when we let Billy's dog loose on dog-shooting day?

Underneath the writing is the drawing of a headless dog. I can feel the blood rushing out of my face and hear my heartbeat pound in my ears.

I jump up and run out the door before the teacher even has time to say my name. I don't stop until I'm in the dog yard. It's eerily quiet. Usually the dogs come rushing out of their houses when they see me. Happy running around in her circle, jumping up and down on the roof of her house. Lightning whining impatiently until I pet him. Acimosis stuffing his nose under my jacket and sneezing. And Cheerio looking out of his house. Two feet in, two feet out.

Today, nobody comes to greet me. Their chains lie motionless in the snow. I can feel my hand clench around the crumpled-up note.

I hear a car door slam and turn around. Poplar Point Family Taxi is parked in front of the cabin. The old man walks down the beaten trail with a big cardboard box in his arms. When he sees me, his eyes light up like he's going to smile, but then he notices the empty houses. A rifle shot echoes through the air. With a dull thud the box hits the snow and tin cans and potatoes roll out.

"Acimosis," he says and my throat chokes up because, in a way, it's all my fault. If I hadn't brought the dogs to his yard, then Acimosis wouldn't have taken off with them on the worst day ever.

I want to scream, but it's like there's no sound in me. I bite my lip. The smell of blood hangs over Poplar Point like the smell of water on a foggy day. I can't escape it. It's everywhere. Even my mouth has that metallic taste.

Another shot.

"Acimosis!" the old man whispers into the sky, like Acimosis is too far away to hear him here on earth.

And Acimosis answers. A quiet whine, high pitched, pleading. It comes from the back door.

The old man and I glance at each other like we just woke up from a horrible nightmare and run around the cabin. Acimosis is leaning against the door, shivering so hard that you can see the door shake. Acimosis wags his tail when he sees us and crawls between the old man's legs.

There are scratch marks on the wooden slats of the door and, when I bend down to bury my face in his thick fur, I notice that one of his toenails is broken. Drips of blood turn the white snow into a deep red.

The old man opens the door. Acimosis bolts inside and crawls under the kitchen table. I take a deep breath and wipe the tears from my cheeks. I realize that my lip is bleeding, which is where the smell of blood must have come from.

I still have a bad aftertaste in my mouth when I leave the yard and sprint down the road.

"Happy! Cheerio! Come!" I only called Lightning "Lightning" in my mind. That I don't even have a name I can call him by makes me sick to my stomach. I don't want him to die without a name.

"Lightning!" I feel better now that I hear my own voice call his name.

"Happy! Cheerio! Lightning!" I run until the pain in my sides gets so strong I have to stop. I call the dog names in between each gasp for air. A car honks its horn and swerves to get around me.

That's when I realize that I'm standing in the middle of the highway. That totally doesn't make sense. Why would I expect to find the dogs here?

And I realize I wasn't really looking. I was just running to get away from what I might find. But that doesn't help. I need to find the dogs. Quick. So I try to think like the dogs. Where would they go? I run to Cheerio's old home but he's not there. I don't expect to see Lightning at his home, but I check anyway. When I round the corner, a shaggy little dog runs past me and then I see the truck. I can't make out the driver, but I see the gun sticking out the passenger window.

"NOOOOOOO!"

The rifle shot ringing in my ears drowns out my scream. I don't look back. My knees are shaking but I keep running.

Happy's not at my home, either. Think! Think like a dog. Maybe they're not in town at all! Maybe they're out in the bush chasing rabbits. I just about laugh with relief when I picture Happy bouncing through the deep snow, stuffing her head in rabbit tracks and running zig-zag here and there.

I decide to go back to the old man's house and check the

MIRIAM KÖRNER

bush behind his dog yard. My mouth is dry; my side feels like someone stuck a knife into it; and my legs are shivering so violently, I think they might give out under me. I need a drink. It's not far to Andy's gas bar, so I cross the road.

And that's when I see her. "Happy! Happy!" Happy drops her chip bag and bounces toward me. She licks my hand like crazy, and I laugh and cry and hug her all at the same time. I don't ever want to let her go, like if I just hang on to her, everything is going to be all right.

But I know I have to find the other two. I glance over Happy's shoulder. Andy is watching me from the deck by the front door. He spits sunflower shells into the snow and then nods toward the old truck behind the pumps. It's got a flat tire and must have been sitting there all winter. There's something under the truck. It's kind of hard to see because the snow around it is too high. "Come, Happy!" I walk to the truck and kneel in the snow.

"Cheerio!" Cheerio looks at me and crawls further away. I stick my hand out and talk quietly to him. He moves his front paws like he's undecided if he wants to come or not. But even if I can get him out, I'm not sure he would follow me. I pull the strings out of my sweater hood and coax Cheerio closer. I pet him under the chin and slowly, slowly move my hand to his collar. I grab it and drag him out. Cheerio tries to pull back under the truck, but I hold him tight and tie the string to the collar. When I walk by Andy, he waves at me.

"Have you seen the other one? He's just about all black with bits of brown?"

"Other one? I thought you didn't have any dogs."

"Well, no, I didn't … but I do now."

I can't really believe that it's not even a few weeks ago since I got Happy and even less since I got Cheerio and Lightning. It's like I've known them forever.

"Have you seen him?"

"No, I don't think so, but I don't pay much attention to the dogs as long as they don't bother my place. The dog shooters have been here a couple of times. I heard a couple of shots, but

I don't know if they got any."

"If you see him, can you ..." I'm not sure what to ask for. Phoning me wouldn't make any sense, because I'll be out looking for Lightning. "Can you maybe keep him safe?"

"I don't want no stinking dog in my store."

"Can you tie him then? To that old truck maybe?"

"I'll see."

"Please!"

"Okay, okay, will do. Now get that dog out of my garbage."

"Happy!" Happy slinks up to me with a KFC chicken box in her mouth and wags her tail shyly. She totally looks like my cousin when she was three and I caught her in our kitchen with both her little hands in the peanut butter jar.

Happy bounces around me as I walk to the old man's dog yard. Cheerio pulls me this way and that at first, but when I start running, he runs next to me with barely a pull on the string. Each time he hears a shot he drops like he got hit by a bullet. I bend down and pet him, and each time we get going again, he runs closer to me. By the time I can see the cabin at the end of the road, his nose is just about touching my hand.

Happy runs ahead into the yard and Cheerio pulls so suddenly that I let go of the string. They are both in Happy's house when I get there. I tie them up and run into the cabin. The old man is sitting on his bed; Acimosis is lying by his feet. He wags his tail when he sees me but doesn't move.

"Have you seen Lightning? The new one?"

The old man shakes his head.

"Happy and Cheerio are back."

He nods again. "I'll look after them. They are safe now. Have a drink. Take a biscuit."

I grab a cup from the table and dunk it into the water pail. I gobble it down so fast that it runs down my chin. I take a biscuit and run out the door. I nearly choke when I try to run and eat at the same time.

So I stop. Where to next? I don't know where to look anymore, but I can't just go back and wait for Lightning to find his way back. A car drives down the road and I stop it.

"Have you seen a black dog?" I ask the guy behind the steering wheel.

"Yours?"

"Yes."

"Well, what did he look like exactly? I just saw one …" He doesn't need to finish his sentence for me to know where he saw it. The man's face is suddenly out of focus and I quickly wipe my eyes.

"He was about this big and he had a Lightning streak on his face and …" My voice breaks up.

"Hey, hey, hey, no worries. The one I saw was a lot smaller. Jump in. We'll look for him." It doesn't take long to drive along all the streets of Poplar Point. There's Main Street with the trading post, the Lakeside Inn, the grocery store, and the Dollar Store. Then there's the trailer park next to the rez, and the new development with all the fancy houses next to the dumpy apartments, where the new teachers stay until they get a job somewhere down south. We even drive by the sawmill just out of town and we check the dump, too. Nothing.

On Makwa Drive, we meet the dog shooter's truck. A brown paw is sticking up from the truck bed. My stomach turns. I squeeze my eyes shut.

"I'll drop you off by the school here." The man gives me a friendly punch on the shoulder as I climb out of the truck. I walk over to the swings and sit down. I rock myself back and forth and think of Lightning and how he was so full of life.

The image of the paw sticking out from the truck bed is stuck in my head. I wanted to stop and look and make sure it wasn't Lightning, but I couldn't. It wasn't him, I tell myself. He's still alive. Please.

The school bell rings and I jump up. The last thing I want is to talk to anybody or have to explain to Mr. Burns why I missed my math test.

But then I think of Justin and how Annika had slipped me the note, and I start to wonder who let the dogs go, and I feel I'm getting angry. It feels kind of good to be mad, better than crying and not being able to do anything about it.

I run into the school. Justin is one of the last ones to leave our classroom. Before he even sees me, I grab him and push him against the wall. I'm surprised that I can just hold him pinched against the wall.

"Where is he?" I yell. "Bring him back! I want him back!"

And then my voice breaks up and all my power drains out of my arms.

"What have you done?" I sob, and then my knees buckle and I lean against the wall and cry. I bury my face in my arms because I don't want to see anybody. I feel Justin's hand on my shoulder but I shrug it off. I just want to be alone now.

"Hey, Jeremy, are you crying because you messed up your math test? Boo-hoo." That's Bob. I don't care what he says.

"Just leave him alone." Justin says. "Get going, Bob. You're never last to leave the school, so what's keeping you now? Nothing to see here."

I hear footsteps disappearing, Justin and Bob talking back

and forth. I take my arm off my face and sneak a look. When nobody is in the hallway, I quickly slip out of the school.

★

I look for Lightning until it turns dark. There weren't any more gunshots after school. It's done. My head feels empty, kind of hollow, as if the place where I carry all my thoughts and feelings is gone.

I walk to the old man's dog yard and lie in the snow between Happy's and Cheerio's circle. Happy licks my face, but when I don't pet her, she just curls up next to me and puts her nose under her tail. I don't know how long I've been lying there. The old man sits with me for a while. He leaves me his jacket before he walks back into the house.

And then I hear Mom's voice.

"Come on, Jeremy, let's go home."

Mom pulls me up gently. I let her lead me home. Her arm is around my waist, and she half carries me up the steps into the house and drops me onto the couch. She covers me with blankets and brings me a bowl of chili. She puts a movie into the DVD player and sits next to me. We both stare at the screen, but I don't think either of us is paying attention to the action.

I glance at her and I can see the blue of the TV reflected on the tears running down her cheeks. I take her hand and lean my head against her shoulder. I'm not sure who's comforting who but, either way, I know it's not working very well.

CHAPTER 19

"Caw, caw, caw!"

The call of the raven wakes me. I try to sit up but I'm tangled in heavy blankets. There's a sudden jerk and then the scratching sound of a toboggan being dragged through the snow. I'm moving.

"Jeremy!" A voice calls.

I struggle out of my blankets and push aside the canvas tarp that covers me. The tarp smells fishy and I'm glad to get rid of it, but the air is cold. So cold that it feels like tiny icicles form inside my nose. The dogs are running fast. They are chasing the raven. The sled bounces over drifts and I'm thrown up and down. I know something is wrong, but I don't know what.

"Jeremy, jump! Jump out!"

I look behind me. A man is trying to catch up to the toboggan. If only I could get to him, everything will be all right, but the sled is going too fast. I start crying. The man becomes a tiny dot on the endless white of the lake. And then I lose sight of him.

Something tickles my cheek. I wipe it and feel the tongue of a little dog, a puppy. He's still tiny. A little fur ball. Yellow.

"Jeremieeeeeee." The voice fades into the distance. There is a strange knocking sound. Like something big, banging from underneath the ice.

★

"Jeremy!" Bang, bang, bang. "Wake up!"

I open my eyes. At first I don't know where I am, and then I realize I'm on the couch in our living room. The only light comes from the clock on the DVD player: 3:16 AM. I'm relieved that it was just a dream, but then I hear the knocking sound again.

"Jeremy!"

Someone is banging on our door. I feel my way to the light

switch and nearly trip over the blankets I'm wrapped in. I open the door and there's Justin. He's carrying something heavy in his arms; it's limp, like a child asleep.

"Lightning?" I ask. "Is he ...?"

"No, he's alive, but he's hurt." Justin steps into the house and lays him carefully on the floor.

"Where ...?"

"Not important now. He needs help. Good luck." Justin steps back and slowly closes the door.

I switch on the porch light and kneel down next to Lightning. A pool of blood forms under his tail. Lightning raises his head and whimpers like he always does when he wants me to pet him. I pet him under the chin and he closes his eyes. He is panting heavily.

"Mom!" I yell. I hear her bedroom door open and she appears like a ghost, in her white T-shirt and with dark rings under her eyes.

"Jeremy, what the ...!" When she sees the motionless dog, she carefully lifts his tail. "He's lucky. The bullet just scraped him. Get some warm water and a clean T-shirt."

Mom cleans up the wound while I stroke Lightning's fur. She rips the T-shirt into strips and makes a bandage. I clean up the floor with the rest of the shirt. Lightning whimpers when I leave him to throw out the rags. Before I go back to him, I quickly fill an empty margarine container with water. He wags his tail when he sees me, but then whimpers even more. It must hurt to move it. He raises his head when I put the water next to him and he drinks greedily.

"Here," Mom says and passes me the leftover hamburger from the chili. We always buy the bulk pack, and then it's hamburger in chili, hamburger in pasta, and hamburger in soup, until it's all gone. I guess tomorrow will be vegetarian. I smile at Mom.

"Thanks." I put the hamburger next to Lightning.

He smacks his lips but doesn't touch it.

"Here, you need this to get strong." I hold out a few bits at a time and he takes them carefully from my hand.

"I'll go back to bed now," Mom says. "When I wake up in

the morning, the last thing I want to see is a dog in my house."

"Mom!" I protest.

"But I guess I don't have a choice." She winks at me. "He'll be fine. He just lost a lot of blood—that's why he's so down. He'll recover fast as long as we keep that bandage tight."

I drag my mattress into the porch and sleep next to Lightning. When I wake up in the morning, he's curled up by my feet on my mattress.

"Lightning! Don't let Mom see you!"

He gets up and stretches lazily like he's saying: Mattress? What mattress?

★

I stay home to look after Lightning. Mom was reluctant at first, but she didn't like the prospect of stepping into dog pooh in our front porch when she comes home, either. Plus, someone has to look after his wound. I change his bandages when I see blood is seeping through.

In the evening, Mom brings some real bandages and some antibiotic ointment from work. He's eating and drinking like a horse and I think he's lots better. I wasn't even sure he would make it, and now he's running around when I let him out for a pee like nothing ever happened.

Well, not like nothing happened. He still yelps once in a while and tries to bite his tail. And he's a lot more skittish than before. Any loud noise and he bolts to hide under the porch steps. But he's over the worst. He just needs time now to heal. So on Friday, I go back to school.

I run home during recess and lunch to let him out, and each time he's waiting for me by the front door. But I know he doesn't sit there all day, because there's a lot of dog hair on our couch.

I'm sitting on the floor, rubbing my hands in Lightning's fur, when I hear someone walk up the front steps. The door opens. It's Justin.

"How is he?" he asks.

"Okay, I guess." I don't want to let Justin in the house,

because I don't want him anywhere close to Lightning. I'm still not sure if it was Justin who let my dogs go.

When I asked him at school where he found Lightning, he didn't want to come out with the story, either. I think he went looking for him. Maybe he felt bad about letting them loose, or maybe just bad because of the argument we had and then the horrible drawing in his note. I don't know. I just don't want to think of Justin as a bad person, but I can't really trust him, either, after all that happened.

So I just tell him Lightning is going to be all right and thanks for his help. I am just about to close the door, when Lightning squeezes passed me and puts his front paws up on Justin. At first Justin steps away, but then he just stands there and looks into Lightning's eyes, and Lightning stares right back. He does his quiet whimper, like he does when he wants me to pet him, and I kind of feel jealous for a second, because I thought it was a special thing between him and me.

But then I see Justin standing there and tears coming into

his eyes. And he doesn't even try to hide it or make a joke about it or anything. He just stands there. And I don't know what to do, but Lightning does, so I leave them there. Just the two of them on the steps outside our house.

CHAPTER 20

It's time for Lightning to go back to the dog yard—at least, that's what Mom says. I wouldn't mind if he slept in my bed and was the first one to say hello when I come home from school, but my opinion doesn't exactly count in dog matters. He still needs his wound cleaned every day, but it's amazing to see how much it's already healed in three days.

I haven't seen the other dogs since Wednesday and I'm looking forward to being with them. Lightning seems to be excited, too. As soon as we step out of the house, he runs ahead of me down the road. Before he gets out of sight, he stops and waits for me. It's as if he's looking out for me. As if he's taking me for a walk and not the other way round.

The dogs start barking even before Lightning reaches the yard. Acimosis comes to greet us by the fence. The fur on his neck stands up and his tail points straight in the air. Lightning returns the rather formal greeting stiff-legged, and then he blasts off to see Happy. Cheerio runs like crazy around his circle and, once in a while, the three dogs collide and rabble-rouse like first graders on their first day outside after a week of indoor recess.

I untie Happy and Cheerio and the dogs run around me in circles, pick up old bones that the ravens have stolen from them, and chase each other. Even Acimosis gets sucked into the game and runs around, bouncing like a puppy. I'm so happy watching them play that I don't notice I'm not the only one.

The old man stands in the open door and grins like he's just won the radio bingo.

"Looks a lot better than I thought," he says.

I feel a little bit guilty, because I only told him that I had found Lightning and that he was shot, and then I was so wrapped up in looking after Lightning, I didn't tell him that it was way better than it looked. But I don't think he minds. What matters is now.

We watch the dogs play until Happy comes to me and licks my hand. I pet her head and, a second later, Lightning is nosing me, and then Acimosis paws at the old man's leg. Even Cheerio accepts a rub under his chin, although I have to stretch out my arm quite a bit to reach him. But that's not important. What's important is that I suddenly feel like I'm part of one big, happy family.

"You gonna go running today?" The old man nods toward the sled. I hadn't thought of it since the incident with Lightning, but now I can't wait to hook them up.

The only problem is it's real cold today. The smoke from the cabin shoots straight up into the air, like the sky is trying to suck up all the warmth. The trees are frosty and the snow on the lake glitters like a million tiny stars. I don't think I ever noticed how nice it looks when it's so cold. Maybe because I usually stay inside on days like this—or maybe I just never paid attention.

Whichever it is, one thing is for sure: I'm not exactly dressed to go out on the lake at forty below zero.

It's like the old man read my thoughts because, while I'm still trying to make up my mind, he passes me a pair of beaver mitts and moose-hide mukluks.

I slip my hands into the mitts and my hands instantly feel like they're wrapped in warm blankets. I don't really want to take them off again to change my boots, but I can't do anything with my hands inside the big mitts. I put the mukluks on as quick as I can. They're not the fancy kind with beadwork and fur and all. They're just plain moose hide on the bottom part and canvas on the top. I slip into the felt liners inside the mukluks and tie the long leather string around my leg just above my ankles.

"I can't believe those are warmer than my Sorels!" I say. The old man smiles. He pulls out a pair of white cotton gloves from his pocket and hands them to me.

"So you don't have to touch them snaps with your bare hands," he says.

"Can Lightning go?"

"As long as his wound isn't bleeding or infected, he can go."

I harness one dog at a time, and then I rub my hands and warm them up in the beaver mitts. It takes a long time before we're ready to go, but at least the dogs are sitting patiently, as if they know everything is a bit slower today—at least until I pull my hook.

The dogs take off so fast, my sled gets airborne when we hit the bank down to the lake. My sled skids sideways, hits a hard-packed drift, and I quickly hunker down and close my eyes, totally expecting to hit the snow. Seconds later, we're on the skidoo track and I'm still standing. I guess the adrenalin must still be pumping, because it takes me a few minutes to realize that the dogs have settled into a less crazy speed and the sled follows behind, nice and steady.

My fingers are cramping. I hadn't realized how tight I was holding onto the handlebar. I loosen the grip. My hands are hot and sweaty and I pull one mitt off at a time to cool them off, but put them back on real quick. The cold really hurts.

The toboggan boards make a kind of grinding noise, like if you pull something through sand. Come to think of it, it must feel the same for the dogs, because they look like they have to pull harder now that the snow is crystally from the cold.

They lean into their harnesses and pull with their heads down. Their backs look rounder now, as if they're using their whole weight to pull forward.

A raven caws above us and, when I look up, I see a sundog around the sun. I try to remember how it is again that we see them. But all I remember is that it has something to do with real cold weather and ice-crystals called diamond dust, and I only remember that because, when our teacher explained it to us in science class, I thought it would be cool if it was actually real diamond dust.

And then I stop thinking altogether. I just watch my dogs running. Cheerio's tongue is flopping while he's running. Where it touches the side of his face there's white foam freezing into his fur. Happy's ears bounce with every step, and Acimosis's ears that usually stand up straight, are laying back. I can't see Lightning's ears. His head is lowered and I think he works the hardest.

All of a sudden, he changes his stride. Until now, his front legs moved parallel and at the same time, kind of like a rabbit running full blast, but now his right front foot moves at the same time as his left back leg. It's like they suddenly switched gears from a fast pace to a more unhurried trot. Are they getting tired? How would I know?

I decide to call it a day and turn around. "*Cha*," I call at the next skidoo track crossing ours.

Lightning looks back. He steps right, but the other dogs just keep going and before he can make a decision we are past the track.

I scrape my snow hook through the snow when I see the next possible turn and bring the team nearly to a stop.

"*Cha!*"

Lightning and Acimosis turn and Cheerio and Happy follow. They start running in their faster gear as soon as we're turned around and back on the home stretch. Maybe they weren't really tired, just saving their energy.

"You are back," the old man says when I walk into the cabin, after unhooking the dogs and tying them to their houses. He fills a cup with tea and passes it to me.

I like how the old man just states things as they are. Like "You are back." It's a fact, but also kind of an invitation if I want to talk.

My mom would say, "You're back already?" There's always a question mark attached to it that requires an answer. I don't really know how to explain it—it's just that with Mom, I feel the need to justify whatever I do, and I don't have that feeling with the old man.

"I wasn't sure if the dogs were tired."

"They had tight lines?"

"I think so."

"Then they weren't tired. They can go far. And if they are tired, you take a break and then they can go far again. And each time you take them out for a run, they get stronger and stronger and you can go further and further."

That makes total sense. It's like the first hockey game of the year. I get tired real quick and my legs and ankles hurt. By the end of the season, I could play hockey all day.

"So if the dogs don't run in the summer because there's no snow, does it mean in the winter they have to start training all over again?"

"Every winter. That's why all the races are in the spring. That's when the dogs are the fastest and strongest. Well, that and because in the past, the trappers would come back in the spring when the trapping isn't so good anymore, but the ice is still good to travel with the dogs.

"My dad used to wait till the last moment. Sometimes we didn't leave till the end of April. We put sled runners under the canoe, and my mother and sisters sat in the canoe with all the gear.

"When the going was good, my dad and me catched a ride, too. If we come into a narrows, we go through the bush. Avoid the thin ice. Sometimes the portage is close to open water if you travel late in the season.

"One time, the dogs ran off the portage and onto the lake and broke through the ice. We couldn't stop fast enough and into the water we went. The canoe was tied to the sled, so we just floated in the water. The dogs turned to swim back to shore—or that's what we all thought they would do.

"But, instead, they tried to climb into the canoe. My sisters screamed and grabbed the gunwales and the canoe tipped over. The water was cold and my sisters screamed even more, and maybe I screamed a little, too. But my dad pulled the dogs and the canoe out and made a fire, and we all dried out our gear and all the furs and everything.

"Luckily it was a warm and sunny day. By the time we were all dry, it was dark. So my dad and I put up a tarp and we lay out spruce boughs and some furs and had a good night's sleep. It never got cold that night, and the next day was maybe the last day anybody could travel. Whoever was still out there had to wait till break-up and come out with the canoe."

I shudder because I can't imagine what it would have been like to end up in the water when the lake is still covered in ice. But then the image of a warm fire and clothes hanging all over the trees around it comes up in my mind. I can almost hear the crackling of the flames, and I imagine helping my dad make our camp real cozy for my sisters and my mom, and then we all cuddle up together. If my sisters would be anything like my cousins Melanie and Jeanette, I would tell them ghost stories and scare them in the middle of the night. I snicker at the thought of it.

And then I suddenly feel empty, because I don't have sisters to scare and I never had the chance to put up a tarp with my dad.

CHAPTER

21

I wake up gasping for air. My hands are holding tight onto the edge of the mattress and my blankets are kicked aside. I had that dream again. Me inside a toboggan. It still doesn't make sense. In my dream, I'm little. Even younger than Isaac. Maybe like the kids that go to pre-school. I feel I should know the voice that keeps telling me to jump out of the toboggan, but I have no idea where from.

I have a stale taste in my mouth. I walk into the kitchen and pour myself a bowl of Frosties. The clock on the microwave reads 10:25 AM.

Mom has left me a note on the kitchen table.

Will go to the craft fair after Church. Not sure when I'm back. There's some leftover lasagne in the fridge. Have a good day.

Usually, I'd be happy she let me sleep in and do my own thing. But today is kind of different. For some reason, I miss her—or maybe not even her, but just someone being here. It's like the silence is too loud. The humming of the fridge gets into my head. I need to get out of the house.

For a moment, I think I'll go to the Christmas sale. It's kind of neat to see people bringing the stuff they made.

Last year, someone made moccasins with the Ice Huskies hockey team logo on them. I thought that was pretty cool. Same lady had some credit card holders with traditional flower designs. I couldn't make up my mind if I should buy Mom the cardholder or a birch-bark basket for Christmas. And then I thought she always likes it if I make stuff for her.

So I looked around to get some ideas of what I could make. Jams 'n' jellies were out of the question. Anything to do with sewing or knitting as well. So I decided on a birch-bark biting. I looked at Mrs. Merasty's patterns of flowers and dragonflies real close. Didn't look any more difficult than the paper snowflakes we made in Grade 3. Instead of folding up the paper and cutting the pattern into it, I would just have to use birch bark and my teeth.

No matter how hard I tried, my teeth weren't cut out to make fancy patterns. Or any patterns at all. I still remember the bitter taste in my mouth, and the birch bark that looked like someone had dropped it on the gravel road and backed up their car a couple times over it.

I ended up seeing Mrs. Merasty the night before Christmas, but she had sold all her bitings. When I told her about my problem, she smiled a toothless smile. How can someone without front teeth make such fine bitings? She showed me, and I found out you use the teeth further back. She let me do a couple of bites, but before I messed it up too much, she finished it, and it looked just as good as her others. It's still standing on our windowsill. Mom bought one of those clear plastic frames at the Dollar Store and we slipped the biting in between, so the light makes the pattern real visible and pretty.

Looking at it now, I see it's not as great as I remember, but Mom liked it. I really should go to the craft fair and see if I can buy her something, but I don't really feel like being in the gym with all these people crowding around the tables, and the smell of smoked hide mixed in with too many people breathing in one room. So I decide to go and see my dogs.

I'm kind of anxious when I near the yard. I relax when I see Acimosis sniff around Happy's circle and Cheerio lying on top of his roof, blinking into the sunshine. Good, everything is as it should be. Only, when I walk around the corner and Lightning's house comes into view, I notice he's missing. I storm into the cabin.

"Where's Lightning? He's not there!" I'm so panicked that I just about trip over something on the floor. "Lightning! What happened?"

"Wound is infected. Your friend noticed." The old man is kneeling by the dog.

"My friend?" I lift my eyes off Lightning, and then I see

Justin by the stove with one of those old tin washbasins in his hand. At the same time, I notice the smell. There's a rank stink coming from Lightning's tail, but there's also something else. A late summer smell. Not real sweet, but not as bad as high-bush cranberries, either. Like the smell that sometimes drifts into our backyard from the clearing where the old school used to be. My stomach tightens when I see Justin. I don't know why he is here or what happened. The only thing I know is I don't want him here. I think he can tell I'm not too pleased to see him. He just stands there with the washbasin in his arms.

"Better get them bandages while they're hot," the old man nods at Justin and then at Lightning. Lightning is staring at me. Like he's complaining I didn't even say hello yet.

"Hey, boy!" I sit next to him and stroke his long fine fur.

"What happened to you?" Justin sets the bowl on the floor and fishes out a rag that's floating amongst a bunch of dried plants.

"What's this?" I ask.

"Medicine to stop infection." The old man carefully takes

the rag from Justin and begins cleaning Lightning's wound. Lightning licks at the rag and the old man's hand.

"Let me," I say, because he's my dog and I don't just want to stand there and watch while Justin does all the helping. I glare at him, while I try to stop Lightning from licking his tail with my left hand and clean his wound with the other.

"I just came to see how Lightning was. I … I thought you were here. I stopped by your place, even called you from under your window. But when you didn't answer, I thought I'd find you here. I … was gonna leave, but then Lightning … he … he … I don't know … he seemed happy to see me?"

It sounds like a question, like he isn't sure if Lightning was happy to see him, but it sounds kind of hopeful, too, like he really wants Lightning to like him. I still wish Justin wasn't here but, now that he is, I can't just send him away. And Lightning does like him, whether I like it or not.

"Can you hold his head, so he isn't licking me while I look after him?" I say and try really hard not to sound unfriendly.

Justin quickly kneels down by Lightning's head and strokes him real careful and real gentle. My stomach is kind of turning, because of the smell and all the yellow pus, but when it's all clean, the wound doesn't look all that bad.

Lightning is happy when we let him back out into the dog yard. I pet Happy and Cheerio, and then I don't know what to do. I just want to take the dogs out for a run, but I don't feel right to just take off and leave Justin. But I don't want him to come, either. Plus, now that Lightning's wound is infected, he probably shouldn't come.

"I have to go," I say. "I need to buy a Christmas present for my mom at the craft fair."

"What are you going to buy her?"

I shrug my shoulders.

"Don't know yet."

"I'll come with you," Justin says. "Got nothing else to do, and maybe there's some hot chicks out there," he adds, like he needs an excuse to come along.

"Okay," I say, and it kind of does feel okay, too. I smile at Justin and he punches my arm, but it's so hesitantly that I can barely feel it through my jacket.

"Maybe we can take your dogs for a spin later?"

"Maybe later. Like ... next weekend?" I know I'm only procrastinating. I'm just not sure if I want to take Justin out, but as we walk down the street and I tell him everything I learned about the dogs, and Justin doesn't make any fun of me, I start to get excited. It feels good to share my dog stories with someone. Maybe it's going to be all right after all.

CHAPTER 22

Justin and I are hanging out in school again. It's a bit awkward, because quite often we don't know what to say, but it's okay. Way better than ignoring each other. I haven't taken him back to the dog yard yet, but it's only Wednesday. Maybe I'll take him on the weekend.

When we walk into our classroom, the teacher tells us there's some sort of problem with the water plant. Bad news is we have no running water. Good news is they're shutting down the school for the rest of the day. I guess they aren't allowed to have it open for health reasons or something. Which I don't quite get. What's the difference if we sit at home without water or in school without water? I guess the toilets might be the issue. Could get pretty nasty if we can't flush. Either way, I don't care—I have a whole day I can spend with the dogs and it's not even 10 AM yet.

"I'm gonna run the dogs," I say to Justin.

"Cool," he says. And then we say nothing.

"Wanna come?" I finally ask.

"Couldn't imagine anything better." Justin grins.

I'm still kind of expecting him to say something mean or hurtful or laugh at me. We're kind of tiptoeing around each other like Lightning and Acimosis. I never know if they'll wag their tails or growl at each other.

★

There's no smoke coming out the chimney when we get to the old man's house, but there are still hot coals in the stove. I throw some more firewood in. This way it will still be warm when the old man comes back and his water pails won't be frozen. I remember when I first discovered that he didn't have running water, and I thought it was kind of back-woodsy. Not on a day like today. He's got no worries about plugged toilets, and I think it must be kind of cool to be able to take care of everything you need—he has his outhouse and his drinking water from the lake. If the power goes out, he wouldn't even know. He's got his candles and oil lamps. I guess you can't complain about nothing good to watch on TV if you don't have one.

While I walk to the shed to get the harnesses, I wonder what it would be like to live like the old man. Would you have to worry less if you are totally independent—or more because of all the extra work?

Justin helps me harness the dogs. I laugh when Acimosis drags him face down into the snow.

"Lift up on his collar, like this," I show him. "If he's got only two legs to pull, he's not so strong."

We decide to leave Lightning at home, because I'm not sure if running him will make his wound worse again, and the old man is not there to ask. Lightning is not happy about that. He runs back and forth at the end of his chain. He whines, howls, barks, jumps up and down. He's going totally nuts—that's how badly he wants to come with us. I don't feel good about leaving him, but I would feel even worse if I'd hurt him by running him.

"Are you sure three dogs can pull both of us?" Justin asks.

I smile. "Just wait."

Justin crawls into the sled bag, and I am just about to pull the hook, when I see that he's just wearing jeans and Sorels and a jacket without a hood. I run back into the cabin and grab a blanket from the old man's bed. I don't think he'll mind, but even if he does, we'll probably be back before he gets home.

★

"Woo whoo!" Justin calls when we bounce over the bank and onto the lake so fast that we're airborne for a second. "I didn't think they could go that fast! Look at that big dog go! What's his name again? The one in the front?"

"Acimosis. Then Cheerio, and Happy is last. She needs to be in wheel so she doesn't get side-tracked by the dogs behind her."

"Wheel?"

"That's what they call the dogs right in front of the sled."

"So you don't have to do anything? It's just up to the dogs?"

"You just hang on. And maybe lean a bit into the inside turns. Wanna try?"

"Ahm … maybe later. I don't want to mess up your dogs."

"Sure, you can run on the way back if you want."

We're both silent, but it's the good kind of silent. The one where you're just happy where you are, and you don't need to prove anything or be cool or think of some joke. The dogs kind of do that to you. Like you're more part of the team if you just say the things they understand, too. Like, "Good dogs."

"Whoa, easy, easy!"

I drag my leg through the snow to slow down the sled, because Cheerio is pooping and I don't want Happy to run over him. Acimosis pulls harder.

"Hey, whoa!"

I throw my hook in and everyone stops.

"Can't let them get away with it, or they just go crazy."

I tell Justin about my first trials and mistrials, and he asks so many questions that I forget to look behind me to check how far we are from town. When I do remember, I can't even see the church tower. Only the smoke of the houses shining bright white against a dark gray-blue sky. It's real pretty because, where we are, it's sunny and the snow looks even whiter.

"*Cha!*" I call. Acimosis jumps left. "No!" I quickly put my hook down. Acimosis doesn't hesitate a second and runs right.

"That's it, good dog!" I call and Acimosis pulls even harder.

"Where you going?"

"Back. Do you want to stand on the running board now?"

"Back? We've barely left. Are the dogs tired?"

"No, but ..." I hesitate. "I promised my mom never to lose sight of the town."

"Oh, if that's the problem, don't worry. I know my way

around here. We can go to Jackfish Narrows or Long Island if you want."

"I don't know."

I mean, I did promise—but Justin is right. She probably just made me promise because she was worried I might get lost. But I don't like the idea of going to Jackfish Narrows. Maybe it's stupid, since it's because of the story the old man told me about the sled breaking through near the narrows. And I know Long Island is right at the other end of the lake. That's pretty far.

"Let's just go straight to those islands over there, and then it's just straight back," I say.

"Whatever. It's just cool to tour around with the dogs."

"*U!*" I tell Acimosis at the next snowmobile track we cross that leads us north again. He immediately turns left. Looks like he doesn't want to go home yet, either. I keep looking back so I can remember the way, but the shoreline is just one even line now, and already I have difficulties seeing where town is. Oh, well, we'll just follow our tracks back.

I focus on what lies ahead. I'm surprised we aren't any closer to the islands yet. They must be bigger and further away than I thought. The dogs fall into their even trot and I watch their arched backs.

When Cheerio tries to bite snow while he's running, I stop the team. Cheerio flops down and eats snow like it's whipping cream. Happy rolls around until she's so tangled in her lines that Justin has to help her out. Acimosis stuffs his whole head into the snow. It sticks to his fur like flour when you're making bannock. Justin and I laugh.

When the dogs are done gobbling snow, they start lunging at their lines. Acimosis is the worst.

"Sit!" I say and he does his butt-two-inches-off-the-ground-pretend-sit.

"I guess they're ready. You wanna try now?" I tell Justin that he has to drag his foot if the dogs stop pulling, so the sled doesn't run into them. And how to tell them to go left and right and straight, and how to make them stop. Then I explain how the snow hook works and how he has to be careful when he puts it in while the dogs are still moving, so it doesn't pull under the toboggan and break his hand. When I'm done explaining everything I can think of, I realize I've talked non-stop for quite a while. In my excitement, I totally failed to notice Justin's worried face.

"Maybe I'll just sit in the sled today," he says.

I didn't want to make him nervous, but I suddenly realize how much I've learned in the past few weeks, and that it doesn't sound as easy as it really is. I'm kind of proud of what I've achieved, but then I feel a bit sad, because Justin always used to be the one who was braver and knew what to do.

If he's not going to try now, he never will, and he'll say dog sledding is stupid. And I don't want that.

"Once you get going, it's not all that complicated. Kind of like when you're trying to ride a bike when you're a kid. It's kind of scary because you think you got no control, but once you figure it out, you can do it with your eyes closed. Besides, I wanna know what it's like to sit in the sled."

I climb into the toboggan and sit on the blanket. Justin has no choice. He pulls the hook and the dogs take off. It's kind of neat to see them from this height; it almost feels like being the wheel dog now. The dogs move their feet so perfectly synchronized, as if they're following a drum beat. For the first time, I notice that their paws throw up snow, and I watch it drift across the trail.

"That's so cool!" Justin calls. "Look at them go, Jeremy! They're all working hard and they're doing it for me."

I smile. I bet Justin is smiling, too. We ride in silence, both with our own thoughts.

It's kind of cooler down here, feels windier, too. I pull the blanket over my legs and wiggle my toes. We're in between the islands now, and snowmobile tracks go all over the place to people's favorite fishing spots. Acimosis isn't listening to Justin's commands, so the dogs just pick their own trail. We come to a stop in a little bay by one of the bigger islands, where a skidoo had turned around.

It's nice to be out of the wind, and the dogs look tired, so we decide to take a break. Cheerio curls up into a ball and puts his nose under his tail. Acimosis falls asleep sitting up, and Happy busies herself with digging a hole in the snow. When she's satisfied with her efforts, she flops into it and then all is quiet. I watch fluffy snowflakes settle on the dogs' fur, and then I stretch my tongue out to catch the cool wet flakes. I haven't done that for a long time, and I kind of grin sheepishly at Justin when I think how stupid it must look to him, but he just smiles back.

"Do you still have your sandwich from this morning?" Justin asks.

I pull my backpack out of the toboggan and pass him half of my frozen peanut butter jelly sandwich. I'm hungry enough I could have eaten the whole thing and then some, but it feels good to share it with Justin just like we used to. It's hard work to bite off little pieces, and once the peanut butter thaws in my mouth, it sticks to my gums. I pull out my water bottle. It's frozen solid.

I chuck it back into the sled and eat a mouthful of fresh snow, instead, but it doesn't really make me any less thirsty. I remember the old man telling me that he would chip out ice with the axe and slowly melt it in his mouth if he was so thirsty that he couldn't wait for the fire to be built and the tea to be boiled.

There's an axe stuck in between the two plywood pieces holding the handlebar together, because the old man wouldn't let me go anywhere without an axe. I didn't say anything, but I remember thinking I wasn't going anywhere, anyway, with or without an axe. I was just doing loops not far from his cabin. For a second, I think about chopping ice, but then I think we're only a couple hours or so from home and I can easily wait that long.

"Let's go home," I say to Justin. He's sitting in front of the dogs and watching them sleep.

"I was just about to have a little snooze myself," he grins and stretches out in the snow. "You got no idea how early I got up this morning," he yawns and closes his eyes.

"Seven-thirty, like everyone else?" I guess. "No … wait … more like eight-thirty, because I recall you hadn't honored us with your presence when the bell rang."

"I hadn't honored you with my presence, and you couldn't imagine in your wildest dreams ... hey!"

I hit him with a snowball before he can finish his sentence and tell me about all the girls he honored. He throws a ball lazily back at me and grins.

"Serious!" he says, but we both know it's a lie, and I don't think either of us minds. It feels kind of good to kid around with Justin like nothing really has changed, except it's even better than before. More honest, I think. But most importantly, I know now he won't hurt my dogs. And I think he really cares about Lightning.

"Let's go back," I say and it's not only because I'm thirsty and I want to be back before the old man comes home and starts to wonder where we are, it's also because of Lightning. He couldn't understand why we left him behind, and his sad howl echoed across the lake for a long time.

★

When we leave the shelter of the island, it feels like a total different world. A furious wind tears at my clothes and blasts snow into my face. I pull my toque off my head before it gets blown away, but I immediately regret it. It's like my brain is being put into a deep freezer, kind of the way you feel if you eat too much ice cream too fast.

Acimosis stops and the dogs turn downwind to escape the fury of the storm. Their tails flutter like flags in the wind. Snow devils whirl across the lake and blur the islands around us. I stare out onto the lake and don't know if I should be fascinated by the strangely beautiful world that surrounds us—or terrified. When I discover I can't make out the shore, I feel fear creep up into my bones. I start to shiver. I'm pretty sure it's not just the cold.

"Holy cow!" says Justin. I guess I'm not the only one scared by the change in the weather.

"We better get home before it gets worse," I say.

"No kidding. Let's get the heck out of here."

"Which way?" I ask.

"Same way we came, doughhead."

"I ... hm ... I'm not sure now—looks so different when you can't even see the islands in the distance."

"Just follow our tracks," Justin says. He sounds slightly annoyed, like I'm stupid or something. I don't have to say anything, because I can tell by the long list of words better not repeated that he can see, too, that our tracks are gone. Blown away like all the skidoo tracks.

"What now?" Justin asks.

"Your guess is as good as mine."

"I'm pretty sure we came this way."

"How sure?" I want to know.

"Geez, I don't know. When we come back from Long Island, we see these islands, I think. And then we just go straight until we see town. But you know how many islands are on this lake."

"Eleven hundred and two."

"What?"

"One thousand, one hundred, and two. I counted them

once on that big map that's hanging in the trading post. You know the one with all the old trapline cabins marked on it?"

"You counted them? You're such a nerd."

It doesn't sound mean or anything. Just like a fact. And maybe I am, but who cares? Because I don't think even Justin minds.

"I was waiting for my mom. They had a big clothing sale and she was trying on all sorts of stuff, and then she met my auntie, and then they started talking forever and I was bored."

"Okay, okay. So there's like a million islands here. But that doesn't help us to get home, does it?"

"Well, at least we kind of know where we are. The islands don't really start till north of town. So if we go straight west, we just have to turn left when we get to shore, and eventually we end up in town."

I can see Justin trying to picture it in his head. "Okay," he says. "Let's do that. Which way is west?"

The sky is gray all over, no way of telling where the sun is. And even if I could, all I know is that the sun sets in the west, and I have no idea if that would be good enough for directions.

"The dogs!" I suddenly remember. "The old man told me they always find their way home! Let's try that." I'm suddenly hopeful again.

"Let's go, Acimosis!"

Acimosis runs straight downwind. I don't think that's where we came from, but the old man also told me to always trust my dogs. We don't get far before Acimosis stops. Without the trail, the dogs have to work a lot harder. Especially Acimosis, because he's breaking trail for everyone else.

"Get out," I tell Justin.

"What? Are you crazy? No way you're gonna leave me here."

"No! Of course not. We need to run next to the sled, so the dogs can pull easier."

"What if they take off on us?"

I hadn't thought about that. Then I remember there's a rope in the sled bag. I tie it to the handlebar and then around my wrist.

"There. Okay, Acimosis," I call.

The dogs take off and, without us, the toboggan rides on top of the snow. They're gone so fast that my arm gets nearly pulled out my socket when they come to the end of the rope.

"Ouch! Whoa!" I fall face down into the snow and the dogs stop.

"Are you okay?" Justin barely manages to get the words out before he bursts out laughing.

At first I'm mad, but then I picture the whole scene like I'm not the one with his face in the snow, and I start laughing, too. It's snowing and storming and we don't know if we'll find our way home, but we roll in the snow, laughing and laughing. Like we need to laugh away all our fears, and then we laugh away all the bad things that happened in the last month, and maybe even years, and then I feel tears coming up and stop laughing. Justin offers me his hand and pulls me up.

"It's gonna be okay. Tonight we'll be sitting at home and laughing some more about how lost we were. Now tell them dogs to go home."

We take turns standing on the runners and running behind. We switch before the one running gets too sweaty. We are in the open part of the lake now, and it's like we're completely swallowed by white nothingness. I can't tell where the lake ends and the sky starts. Acimosis fades in and out like a ghost, but the dogs are running like they're on a mission. I'm sure it's just another hour or so and we'll be home. Suddenly the dogs run even faster.

"Jump on!" But they're going too fast now. I stop for Justin and he drops into the sled like it's his living room couch.

"What's up? How come they're going so fast suddenly?"

"I think we're on our old trail. And see! There's the shore. I can see trees!"

The trees slowly take shape, and it feels like they're moving toward us and not us toward them. I know it's just an illusion, but it's still kind of cool to see.

"I don't think that's the shore." Justin interrupts my thoughts.

"What?"

"It's an island."

"There are no islands in front of town."

"I know. But that doesn't change the fact that ..." Justin doesn't finish his sentence. The dogs come to a halt.

"We're in big trouble now," Justin says as Happy settles down in the hole she'd dug earlier that day.

We have run in a circle.

CHAPTER 23

"I guess there's no choice. We'll have to stay here for the night."

Saying it out loud doesn't make it any less scary. I can't believe this is real and I can't imagine spending the night out here. It sounded like a cool adventure and kind of fun when I listened to the old man's stories. But it's a little different when you're standing in a blizzard and it's about to get dark, and the snow has drifted at least two feet high against the shore, and you just don't have any idea what to do, except you know somehow you have to make a fire and get enough wood to keep it going. I guess this isn't how Justin had planned to spend his evening, either.

"Staying here? For the night? Are you crazy? I'm half froze already. By morning I'm gonna be so stiff, you can use me as a toboggan board." Justin hugs his own shoulders and jumps up and down.

"We just build a fire."

"Great. Got some gasoline and matches?"

"No, but I got a flint."

"You gotta be kidding."

"No," I say and stomp a trail to the shore. I use my boots to clear a spot and then start to collect dead branches. Justin just stands by the sled and watches me.

The snow is deep in the bush, not so deep you can't get anywhere without snowshoes, but deep enough that walking is tough and I can't find twigs under the snow. So I have to gather wood from the fallen trees that got hung up before they hit the ground. I find birch bark and old man's beard and, when I've got everything ready, I sit down with my flint. I try to shelter the birch bark from the wind and the snow, but it's futile. My little birch-bark bowl fills with snowflakes. This isn't going to work.

"Try this." Justin passes me a lighter and his math book. I take the lighter and manage to get the fire going without tearing up his book.

"Too bad," Justin says.

"What's too bad?"

"Well, you know, I always thought this thing was absolutely useless and, for a second here, I thought I was wrong." Justin waves his textbook at me and smiles. "So we're gonna do the survivorman thing, then? Build some sort of shelter, set some rabbit snares?"

"I guess so." I hadn't really thought that far. Fire was the only thing I could think of. I'm kind of relieved when Justin gets all excited about building a shelter, but I'm not sure if we can actually do this. Survive, I mean.

★

The flames of the fire flicker so bright that everything else around us seems even duller. Such a contrast between the light orange and the dark gray. That's when it hits me.

"It's getting dark. We have to hurry."

"What are we going to do?"

I realize Justin is better with words than actual doing.

"Take the harnesses off the dogs and pull the toboggan up here for starters. Maybe we can sleep in it or use it for shelter." It feels good to be the one telling him what to do for a change.

"I'll start with the harnesses." Justin walks toward the dogs, and Happy barks happily when she sees Justin coming.

"Shall I let them loose?" Justin asks.

"Sure. They can warm us when we go to sleep."

"They won't run home?"

"Not when we're that far from home. I've taken them for walks a couple of times. They always stick around until we get close to the yard. Then there's no holding them." I never really thought about that. It's kind of strange because, if they're a runaway team, they just keep going no matter what you say, but if they're loose, they stick around close.

As soon as the dogs' harnesses are off, they mingle around me and the fire.

"Hey, hey! Stay back! You're kicking snow into the fire!"

I walk away from the fire and the dogs follow me. They stomp on my feet and press against my legs.

"Yes, you're good dogs."

Usually, I like when they come to me like that, but now I don't have patience for them. I'm happy when they start exploring the bush close by and seem to forget about me.

"I think we should try to remove more snow; it's melting into the fire." I use my boots to drag it away, and Justin finally finds a use for his math book.

"Makes a fine shovel," he grins. I'm glad Justin is here, even though he's the one who got us here in the first place. He makes it sound like some fun adventure.

"We need more wood for the fire and spruce boughs for our shelter. Lots of spruce boughs."

Justin stomps into the bush and breaks off dead twigs and green boughs. We've got quite a pile now, but then I don't know what to do with them. All we have is rope and the blanket. We could set up a makeshift tarp or we could just use the blanket for warmth.

In the end, we decide to prop up the toboggan on its side for a windbreak, and we pile the spruce boughs underneath for our bed. Happy thinks it's hers, and she turns in tight circles and moves the boughs with her paws until she has a bed to her liking. She flops down with a smile on her face.

Acimosis pees on the toboggan and lies down next to her. Cheerio makes his own bed under a spruce tree. I'm a bit worried that I won't be able to catch him tomorrow, but at least he's sticking around close to the other dogs.

Justin and I sit down on the spruce boughs with the dogs between us. It's pitch black around us. I'm tired, cold, and hungry.

"What was that?" Justin suddenly jumps up. "Did you hear that grumbling?"

I can feel my heart pound in my ears and listen into the darkness.

MIRIAM KÖRNER

"There it is again." Justin's voice sounds slightly panicked.

I laugh.

"What?" Justin asks.

"It's my stomach," I giggle, even though I don't think it's real funny. If this storm blows for days, we'll need food.

"Don't do that!" Justin punches me hard enough that it actually hurts.

"I didn't do it on purpose. I'm hungry!"

"Me, too," Justin says, and then he fiddles in his pocket and passes me half a piece of chewing gum. "And I'm cold."

I shake the snow out of the blanket and push Happy over until there's enough room for Justin and me to sit between the dogs. We wrap the blanket around us and stare into the flames.

"Would be all right if we had a couple of wieners to roast," Justin says.

"Or a nice trout," I suggest.

"Or chicken wings with fries."

We both giggle.

"Or my Mom's leftover stew," I add. And then we say nothing.

"Do you think they'll be looking for us?" I try to glance at Justin without him noticing it, which is kind of hard when you're wrapped in the same blanket.

"Probably," he says.

But neither of us dares to ask the next question out loud. Will they find us?

★

There are lots of coals in our fire now. The snow is melting off my mukluks and I'm worried my feet will get wet, so we move the toboggan back a bit, but now my back is too cold. We stick the last wood onto the fire and then play paper, scissors, rock. Loser has to get more wood.

It's me. I stumble through the dark, trying to remember where the dead pine tree was. Once I leave the light of the fire behind, my eyes adjust and it's actually not as dark as I thought. I look up into the sky and there's moonlight shining through the clouds. It's kind of hazy, but it still makes me hopeful. Maybe the storm will ease off?

I find the pine tree and start breaking branches off. They break with a snap and each time I startle myself. I listen into the silence after each snap. I hear the fire crackling. It's a comforting sound. But I also hear a squeaking sound. Like something is moaning. Something not human.

I stand still and hold my breath. I don't want whatever it is to know I'm here. It's somewhere behind me, screeching and squeaking like the rusty swing by the picnic tables in the park.

Then I realize what it is: trees rubbing against each other in the wind. I should be relieved, except I'm not really believing it. I mean, it's the total logical explanation, but I think maybe my brain is just tricking me to look for the logical explanation to calm me down—but what if it's not? I hear a branch snap. My heart suddenly pounds three times as fast. I drop the firewood and run as fast as I can back to our camp.

"Found no wood?"

Justin is lying under the toboggan with Acimosis as a pillow and Happy as a foot warmer. He actually looks comfortable. Relaxed. I listen in the dark, and there's no doubt now that it's just trees rubbing.

"Just came to get the axe," I mumble, "trying to get some bigger stuff."

"Want help?" Justin offers and yawns at the same time.

"Sure!" I say relieved and then feel silly. I can handle this on my own. "Ah, never mind. We only have one axe, anyways." I stomp back on my old trail, and then chop off a huge branch from the tree and drag the whole thing back to the fire. The fire shines on a dead standing tree just past the sled. I chop that off, too.

I work like crazy, because doing something helps me to not think—or at least just to think of the things that need to be done right now. I have to focus real hard to hit the tree I want to cut, with my axe at the same spot, over and over, until I can kick it off with my boot.

When we have a big wood pile, I'm so hot that I sit at the

edge of the fire by Justin's feet. I lean against the curl of the toboggan and Happy wiggles around until her head rests on my lap. I play with her ears and let the soft fur glide through my fingers, until my hands are getting cool and I slip my beaver mitts back on. They're so cozy, it feels like my hands are in bed.

I'm a little boy again. Inside the toboggan. It's so cold that I climb deep into the sled bag. I crawl right under the blankets with the puppy, but I'm still cold. Very cold. And tired. So tired, so cold. I want to close my eyes, but before I can fall asleep, the puppy licks my face.

The fire has burned down and I'm shivering. Happy is licking my face. I get up and throw more wood into the fire. Justin pokes his head out from under the blanket and watches me.

"Did you sleep?" I ask Justin.

"I don't think so. Too cold. You?"

"I had this dream. It's kind of weird, because it kind of feels so real, but it doesn't make any sense. And I keep having the same one, but it's a bit different each time, like it kind of continues. Do you know what I mean?"

"Not really. What's it about?"

"I'm around three years old and I'm inside a toboggan. It's all cozy and comfortable, and I kind of know everything is good. Like it's supposed to be. There's a little puppy with me. He's cute and I'm kind of happy. Then something goes wrong but I don't know what it is. All I know is I hear this voice calling. It tells me to jump out of the sled, but the dogs are going fast and I'm scared. And I cry. And then I get cold. Real cold."

"And then?"

"That's it. At least till now. Weird, no?"

"I don't know. Aren't all dreams weird?"

"Do you have dreams like that?"

"Not with the dogs and stuff. But I had one that kept coming back. Except it was exactly the same one over and over again."

Justin is quiet and I'm not sure if he will keep talking, but I don't want to let the moment pass. I ask him what his dream was about. Justin and I never really talk like this. Maybe girls do. I guess the closest was at the hockey game, where I saw the shooting star. Maybe it's got something to do with it being dark and the whole world around us disappearing into the shadows. It feels good to talk about things we usually never share.

"I'm just a little kid in my dream, too. But older than three, I think. Yes, because in my dream, I have this little pocketknife my dad gave me. He gave it to me for my fifth birthday and I loved it. I carried it everywhere."

I look at Justin. The reflection of the flames dances over his face. He's curled up in his blanket with his knees pulled up to his chin. I know it's because he's cold, but he looks a bit like a little boy, even though he's got a lot more hair above his lip than me. Justin sighs and then he continues his story. His voice is so quiet, I can barely hear it above the crackling of the fire.

"In my dream, I'm hiding behind the woodpile and I'm

waiting for someone or something to come around the corner. I have my knife in my hand and I tighten the grip, because I know I'm going to use it. And then my mom calls me, and I put my knife back into my pocket and run into her arms."

I can feel a shiver go down my spine and I don't really know what to say.

"Do you still have that dream?"

"No. It stopped about the time my uncle Gord moved out. I remember my mom and Uncle Gord having a big argument. I was outside but I heard dishes flying, and then my uncle came out and my mom yelled at him to never, ever set foot in her house again. And he hasn't."

Justin pokes around the fire with a stick. "But I got this other dream, and I still got that. I'm running as fast as I can, but somehow I don't move. I try to run faster but, with every step, I land exactly at the same spot again. There's a wolf behind me and I know he's catching up. I turn around and the last thing I see is his mouth and sharp teeth. Then it's dark and I smell stale breath, like something decaying, and I can't get any air and I wake up screaming."

Justin looks at me for the first time since he started talking. He must have noticed that look of horror on my face.

"Not the kind of story you want to hear on a dark night like this, eh?" He grins.

I smile back. "At least the wolf ate you and not me."

A stick hits me on my head. I totally deserve that. I know it wasn't what I should have said, but I got no idea what to say or what to make of his dreams, so it's just easier to kid around.

"I still got my knife." Justin fiddles in his pockets and chucks it over to me. It's a key-chain thing with the SaskPower logo on it. We both know it's totally useless and we both know it's not the point.

"Let's get some sleep so we can try to get out of here as soon as it gets light. It's not snowing anymore. If we just get going somewhat in the right direction, I'm sure someone will find us."

"It's too cold to sleep," Justin replies.

"Let's race down to the lake and back until we're real warm and then crawl under the blanket," I suggest.

We run into the night and try to push each other over. Acimosis and Happy run around us, barking like crazy, and even Cheerio runs along a little ways off to the side. We're giggling like little boys and it's almost fun.

"We'll be all right, you know," I say, and I don't mean just surviving the night.

"I know," says Justin. And then we crawl under the blanket. I lie awake for a long time, but sleep will not come.

"Jeremy," Justin says. "There's one more thing. The dogs … the day of the shooting …"

I know what he's going to say, and I guess I kind of knew all along.

"It's okay," I say. "I mean, it wasn't okay then, but I'm okay with it now. They're all alive and you did save Lightning, after all."

"I'm sorry, really. I guess, I … I didn't want you to spend so much time with them, but I guess I wasn't thinking, or maybe I was and got it all wrong, and then I saw your face and how worried you were, and then I went looking for Lightning and I found him, and then I realized what I had done and … and … Lightning, I couldn't stop thinking about him, and then … he just looked at me like he understood everything. Even the things that I didn't."

"He really likes you," I say.

"Thank you."

★

I must have dozed off, because the fire burned down again and I'm shivering. Happy is whining quietly and Acimosis is looking down to the lake. His ears are standing up and he looks tense. And then I hear it. A long mournful howl.

"Justin! Wake up!" I kick him with my mukluk and sit up.

"What is it?" He's instantly wide awake—or maybe he hasn't slept at all.

"Wolves!" I whisper. We both listen into the night, and there it is again. The dogs have heard it, too. All three of them are staring into the night, and then they answer back.

"Shh ... Shut up!" I whisper, but the dogs howl even louder. Each time they take a break, the wolves howl. Each time it sounds closer—or is it just my imagination? I sure hope so.

Suddenly, Happy barks and Cheerio runs in the direction where the howling came from.

"Cheerio! NO!" Cheerio hesitates.

"Hold Happy and Acimosis, Justin!" I carefully crawl toward Cheerio. "Come here! Atta good boy!" I talk as happy and cheery as I can. You have to believe it's going to happen, I tell myself.

"Come here, boy! It's best for you, believe me." I try again. And sure enough, he comes! I grab him by his collar and walk him back to our campsite.

"We need to make the fire bigger and ... where's the axe?" I stumble around the fire, holding onto Cheerio with one hand and throwing all the sticks we have left into the fire with the other. It takes a while before the branches burst into flames. The light makes me feel safer and yet, behind the small circle of fire, lurks the darkness with all its known and unknown dangers.

I cling to the axe and listen into the dark. I hear the howl one more time, and the dogs get restless and pull on their collars, and then it's quiet.

"I think it was just one," I say. "Maybe he left."

I'm not even convincing myself, and then everything goes real quick. I hear branches break and suddenly I see eyes glowing in the dark, real close now, and then the wolf runs toward me, and I let go of Cheerio and raise my axe, and then Justin screams and grabs the axe handle before I can swing it.

"It's not a wolf! It's not a wolf!" he screams, and it takes my brain a long time to realize the NOT, even though in real time, it could have only been seconds. And then Lightning is all over me, and the dogs run around licking his nose like they, too, are happy to see him.

"How did you find us?" I ask him. Lightning wags his tail.

"I missed you, too," I say and rub him behind the ears. "He must have got loose and followed our trail! I wonder if he'll find the way back, too." I look at Justin and I can see he's just as excited as me.

"Let's try," says Justin and flips the toboggan over. Lightning is already running back to the lake.

"Hey, wait!" I call. Lightning stops and watches us. I grab Happy's harness and I'm just about to slip it over her neck, when Lightning noses me.

"Hey, no! That's Happy's harness. You can just run ahead loose, okay?"

As if he had heard what I said, he runs down the trail toward the lake. He stops at the same spot and barks. Then he runs to Justin and scratches his chin with his paw. Once more he barks and then runs ahead.

"I think he wants to show us something," Justin says.

"The way home, I hope!" I say and hook up the dogs.

It doesn't take long, and we bounce down the trail to the

lake. The sky is clear now and the moonlight shimmers on the fresh snow. The dogs run fast, like they always do when leaving the yard. Lightning runs ahead, and the dogs work real hard to try to keep up with his pace. But we don't get very far. The dogs suddenly stop and, in the moonlight, I can see Lightning sitting down next to a dark lump in the snow.

"Jack!"

It's the first time I ever used his name, but I don't have time to think about that. I kneel next to the old man. His knees are bent kind of awkward because he's wearing snowshoes. I take them off. I don't know what else to do. I'm too scared to touch him, but I know I have to.

"Wake up!" I say and shake his shoulders.

He opens his eyes. A smile lights up in his face when he sees me. He stretches his hand out and feels my cheek like he has to touch me to believe that I am real. A tear rolls over his cheek.

"Jacob," he says. His voice sounds raspy. "You're alive. All is good now." And then he closes his eyes.

"NO!" I call out.

The old man feels for my hand and squeezes it, but he doesn't say any more. Even in the moonlight, I can tell that his lips are blue.

"Justin! We have to do something!"

Justin kneels next to me.

"He's freezing!" I yell in panic.

"I don't think so—he took his coat and mitts and every-thing off."

"Isn't that what happens right at the end? When you're freezing to death? You feel all cozy and warm, and then you take off your clothes and ..."

"I don't know. Maybe he was just hot from walking."

"He's not hot now." I feel his ice-cold cheek. "We have to get him back to the fire."

"No, we have to get help!" Justin says.

How? I think. I pick up the old man's snowshoes, and then

I drop them again when I see his jacket in the snow. I dust the snow off his jacket, but then I don't really know what to do with it, either.

"Jeremy! What are you doing?"

"I …" I don't know what I'm doing. That's the problem. Get the old man to the fire or home? Either way, we have to get him into the sled.

"Help me," I say to Justin and grab the old man under his arms. Carefully, we lift him into the sled.

"Jacob," the old man mumbles when I put his jacket back on and wrap him into the blanket. I rub his arms and legs and chest as fast as I can, hoping this will help to warm him up.

"Back to the fire or home?" I ask.

"Home!" says Justin. And Lightning barks at us from down the trail.

"Let's go, then!" I say, but I'm scared that this might be a mistake. It's too cold in the sled and we don't know how far we are from home. We should stop and warm up by the fire. That's what he taught me. Again and again. But I'm also relieved that we're moving. I just want to get going, be home. I couldn't face sitting with the old man by the fire doing nothing, not knowing if he will live, and just waiting till someone finds us. *If* someone finds us.

His snowshoes have made a good trail for us to follow, but the going is still slow. Justin and I run along, taking turns, with short breaks on the running board. We pick up the old man's mitts and fur hat and dress him like you would a little child. He slips in and out of consciousness. When he's awake, he talks softly to Jacob in Cree.

"Who's Jacob?" Justin asks while he's taking a breather on the running board.

"My dad," I gasp in between breaths. "His name was Jacob," I add when it's my turn on the running board.

We pile our own jackets on top of the old man and loosely lay them over his face, so his breath can help to warm him up. I lift it every once in a while to make sure he's got enough air.

It feels like we're barely moving at all. The shoreline ahead of us doesn't seem to get any closer and, when I look back, I can still see the silhouette of the island we came from. The toboggan doesn't want to stay on the old man's snowshoe trail. Each time it ends up in the deep fresh snow, I have to push and pull to get it back on the trail. How did they do it in the olden days?

The dogs are moving slower and slower and, to make matters worse, Justin and I have to wait up for each other because we are too out of breath to run anymore. We try both of us standing on the runners, but the dogs slow to a stop each time we do.

We keep running until we both throw up. The further we travel, the more blown in the trail becomes, until only Lightning seems to know where we're going.

And then he stops, too. I look up and there's something next to Lightning—it's a canvas bag. A backpack. The old man must have dropped it here. We rummage through its contents. There's a thermos bottle and beef jerky and pilot biscuits! We fall over the food like hungry squirrels. I pour a cup of tea for the old man and get him to drink a couple of sips, but then he shakes his head.

"Hot makes you too cold."

I'm not sure what he means, but I throw some snow into the cup and he takes another two sips.

Justin and I each drink a cup, and then I have a closer look at the other things in the pack to see if there's something else we can use. I pull out a hatchet, toilet paper, a candle, and matches—and Lightning's harness!

With Lightning helping us to pull, one of us can stand on the toboggan now. I have one foot on the running board and pedal with the other to help the dogs. When I look back, I see Justin quite a bit behind. I wait for him to catch up. The dogs impatiently jerk on their lines. Justin walks up to me and bends over with his hands on his knees. He pants like a dog.

"That's it for me! I can't run anymore." He wipes his sweaty forehead.

"You take the sled, then."

"No, you go. Just leave me that last cookie and go. I'll be fine. See that red glow? Those must be the lights of town, don't you think? Can't miss it now. Besides, I got your tracks to follow."

"Okay," I say. I don't feel good about leaving Justin, but I know we don't have a choice. I've no idea how much time we have left before the old man ... I don't even want to finish my thought. We're moving too slow with one of us running behind.

"Just don't forget to send someone out with a skidoo to get me!" he yells as I'm taking off. "And tell them to bring a couple of beer and some smokes while you're at it!"

I wave to him as I leave and smile. He's still the old Justin. But also different. In a good way.

24
CHAPTER

The dogs are moving slow but steady now. It feels like they could go on forever and ever. Across the frozen lake toward the dimming lights of town. Night is fading away but daylight has not yet arrived. I don't remember if I've ever been out during this time of day. I must have. I just never noticed it before—I mean the stillness. It almost feels unreal, like being in a vacuum.

The dogs and I, we don't have a shadow, like we don't really exist. Everything appears out of focus, as if somebody had tried to make a landscape painting and, instead of painting each tree and each house, it's all thrown together in one streak. I pinch

myself to make sure I'm not caught in a dream or nightmare—
I'm not sure which.

Suddenly, there's a buzzing noise in my head. I can't make
sense of it, until I see bright white lights. Skidoos.

"Hey, here! I'm here!" I wave my arms like crazy. The lights
swerve toward me and, a minute later, two skidoos stop next to me.

"Are you okay?" someone yells over the engine noise.

I nod. The voice sounds familiar. But I'm too tired to make
sense of things. I feel tears well up and I don't know why. I
know I'm safe now but, for some reason, I'm not ready to get
back into town.

"Justin is still out there." I nod behind me.

The two drivers talk to each other and one skidoo follows
my tracks back out onto the lake.

"You're okay to follow me?" the other one asks me. "You're
just about there. See the fire?"

Again I nod. I'm kind of relieved to see the taillights of the
skidoo race ahead. I run up to Lightning and hug him real tight.

"Thank you, Lightning." And then I think if I hadn't named him already, I'd call him Storm Finder. I pet all the dogs as I go back and jump onto the running board. Last, I put my hand on the old man's shoulder.

"We're home now," I tell him.

The old man doesn't reply, but he puts his hand on mine, and that's how we arrive at the shoreline.

All of a sudden, there are people everywhere. Mom is running out onto the ice to greet me. She hugs me so tight, I can barely breathe. Over her shoulder, I see that Uncle Charlie and someone whose name I don't know wrap the old man in a blanket and carry him toward his cabin. There's a big bonfire by the shore, and more and more people come running to hear what happened.

And then the skidoo with Justin arrives and people rush over to Justin. We nod at each other. Justin quickly waves to me, before he turns to the crowd.

"Someone got a shot of whiskey? I sure could use some today."

There's laughter and the people gather around the fire to

MIRIAM KÖRNER

hear Justin's story.

I look at Mom.

"I'm so sorry. It was all my fault. I should have never …"

"Shh …" Mom says. "Let's get you warmed up first."

I suddenly realize how cold I am. My teeth chatter uncontroll-
ably and my hands are nearly too stiff to pull the snow hook.

"The dogs," I say. "I need to look after the dogs."

Mom nods and I run up the hill and into the yard. Smoke rolls
down from the chimney and drifts between the doghouses into the
bush. It looks like fog in the early morning sun. My hands shiver so
badly that I can't get the heavy leather collars over the dogs' heads.

"Let me."

I didn't hear Justin coming but I'm glad he's here.

"They'll need food and water and …" I tell Justin.

"I know. My cousin's got some spoiled moose meat in the
freezer. He's already getting it. And they have a teapot by the
fire; someone will warm up some water. Just go inside. He …
he'll want you there."

"Thanks," I mumble real quick before the tears get hold of me again. I turn toward the cabin door, but then I feel a hand steering me toward the road.

"We're going home. That's the last time you'll set foot in this yard."

"But, Mom! He ... he saved us! If it wasn't for him, we'd still be lost on one of those islands!"

"If it wasn't for him, you would have never been out there in the first place!" she counters.

"If it wasn't for ME," I correct her. And then I tell her everything, right from the first meeting when I was kind of creeped out by the old man, because I thought he knew me somehow or mistook me for someone, and how he didn't let me go out with the dogs until he knew I could look after myself in the bush, and how it was me that had broken the promise and traveled too far, and how Lightning had found us ...

... and then I can't say anything no more, because the memory of finding the old man lying on the ice is suddenly too strong and I don't even know if he will be okay …

… and I have to bite my lip real hard so I don't start crying, and then I hear Mom sniffling, too. She gently steers me into the cabin.

The warmth hits me like a wall. I stumble and Mom steadies me. Two men get up from the kitchen table and leave when they see my mom and me.

An old woman takes two big rocks off the stove and wraps them in towels. She carries them to the bed and places them under the old man's blankets. She talks to my mom before she leaves, but I can't understand what she says. My mom nods and leads me to the kitchen table. I'm not sure I can keep my balance, so I slouch down onto the floor and lean against the log wall right next to the stove. Someone has brought a pile of blankets and Mom uses them to make a bed for me on the floor.

"Take your wet clothes off," she says.

The last thing I see are my PolarTech snow pants dripping from the ceiling next to the old man's wool pants.

CHAPTER 25

Sunshine is tickling my nose when I wake up. It takes me a second to realize where I am.

My mom is sitting on the floor, her head resting on the old man's chest. The old man is awake. He strokes my mom's hair, ever so slightly, like you would stroke a bird with a broken wing. He's all teary-eyed but he looks kind of peaceful. Like things have finally fallen into place.

My hip is sore. I guess I haven't moved an inch the whole time I was sleeping on the floor. When the old man sees I'm awake, his smile broadens and he motions me to come.

I tiptoe over to his bed and take his other hand. My mom

wakes up, and it is as if a shadow falls over the old man's face. He looks like he always does since I met him. Worried or sad. Like someone whose happiness has been taken away a long time ago.

"Jeremy," my mom mumbles and sits up. She tousles my hair like she used to when I was young, and like I had told her a million times not to do anymore. But today I don't mind. I smile at her. She squeezes my hand and then she kind of taps the old man's hand, like you would touch a burner to see if it is turning hot. As if she's scared to get burned.

"I'm sorry, Jack," she mutters, and then she rubs her face real hard as if to stop the tears from coming. "I … I just didn't want to lose him, too! I thought if I just kept him away from you, he … he wouldn't … I …"

"Marie," the old man says. He takes Mom's hand into his and holds it tight. And then my mom's tears start to run. Silently, like the water in spring when all of a sudden the ditches fill up and you have no idea where all that water comes from.

"I miss him every day," my mom says. "I know it doesn't

make any sense, but I never forgave him for leaving us. I ... I know it was an accident, but it was so unfair.

"Jeremy was a baby and I was at home. Alone most of the time, because he was gone. With the dogs. Checking nets. Skinning furs. In the bush. Always in the bush. I ... I blamed you, because he always said, 'Dad is getting old. I'd better give him a hand.' But deep down, I knew better. He loved the bush. Like you. Like ..."

"Like Jeremy," the old man finishes her sentence.

And then it totally hits me. I mean, it wasn't hard to figure out who they were talking about, but it feels like watching a movie where, at first, you don't have any idea what it's about, so you don't really care. Then you get sucked into feeling for the characters and you want things to be okay for them. I never watched a movie where I find out in the end that the main character is my own grandfather, so it's all a bit confusing.

"It ... it wasn't a car accident, then?" I say.

Mom looks at me surprised. "That's what you thought?"

I'm too shocked to be mad at her for never telling me, and suddenly all the dreams start to make sense.

"He … he was out with the dogs, wasn't he? And I was there with him. In the sled."

Now both Mom and the old man look surprised.

"What … what happened?" I ask and then I cover my ears, because I'm not sure if I want to hear. If I'm ready for it. Mom and the old man look at each other. Then Mom nods ever so slightly.

"It was a day just like yesterday," the old man starts—and pauses. He stares out the window, as if he's searching somewhere out there for the story he's about to tell. I take my hands off my ears.

"The net, it was in for two days already. Way out by Pickerel Bay. Jacob, he wanted to go check it. We always go together. So much easier with two.

"But I told him to wait. 'There's a storm coming,' I said.

"'Then we'll take it out before,' he replied. It's no good to leave the net in, but it's no good to be caught by a storm. We argued. He wants to go on his own. He brings you in the cabin and says, 'Make yourself useful, at least. Look after your grandson.'

"But I was mad. I brought you outside and said, 'You take your son home and make yourself a cup of tea. We go tomorrow.'

"He didn't listen. I watched him from the window. He hooked up the dogs while you were playing with the puppy. When he put you into the sled, you cried and stretched out your arms for the puppy. So he put it into the sled with you and then he was gone."

Tears pool in the old man's eyes.

"The dogs came home without him. I don't know what happened, why he lost his team, but I knew this wasn't good. I went looking right away, but the storm was so bad, I couldn't find his tracks. It took two days before we found him. It was too late. He was out in the open part of the lake. There was lots of new snow. Lots of slush. He had wet feet and nowhere to go to make a fire. He must have chased after the dogs, because that's where you were. In the sled and not with me.

"'Look after your grandson,' were his last words, but I didn't."

I suddenly miss my dad. All the things we could have done together.

And my mom. I ... I never realized how much she loved him. And how hard it must be to look at me and see him in me, and know, at the same time, she will never see him again.

And the old man—he wasn't allowed to see his own grandchild. But I'm also mad, because I have a grandfather I never knew and a dad who would understand how I feel about the dogs and ... then I feel really sick and I want to run, just run, but I can't move.

"I didn't jump. That day ... I remember. He told me to jump, but his voice, it scared me, he ... he sounded so scared, and then I was scared and then I ... couldn't jump."

"Jeremy!" My mom holds me and swings me back and forth like I'm three years old. "It wasn't your fault. It was nobody's fault. It was an accident, okay?" She says it like it's not a fact, more like a deal. A deal we all three have to make, so we can believe in it. Not blame each other. Not blame ourselves.

"Okay?" she asks again.

I shake my head.

"How can it be okay?! He's dead! It's never going to be okay." I run out the door, and then I don't know where to go, and then Lightning howls real sad like he's crying with me. I let the dogs go and run toward the lake.

"Jeremy!" my mom yells.

And then the old man's voice. "Marie, let him go."

I quickly glance back and I see them standing together by the door. My mom looks so lost, so tiny, that I feel my throat choke up all over, and I start to run.

The dogs bounce around me and we run onto the lake. The fresh snow is glittering like a million tiny stars in a pure white sky, and I feel a cold wind through my nose, and my thoughts begin to shrink until they're small enough that they fit into my head again ...

... and I think about my dad and how he had known

Yellow Dog, and then I think about all the stories the old man told me from when he was a boy and how they seemed so far away in the past, but not anymore, because I know there will be a lot more stories about my dad, and maybe even about me, and that everything is linked together, and maybe I am who I am because of my dad and because of the old man, who is my grandfather …

… and I think that I'm so lucky to have a grandfather like him and that my dad was lucky to have had a dad like him, and even my mom is lucky, although she didn't see it for so long.

And then I think of Justin and the dogs and the camp fire, and how it would be fun to do it again, but maybe this time with a map and some food, and I picture us sitting by the fire and picture my dad there with us, and I'm glad to have a dad that would have taken me out camping, and then I'm out of breath from running and fall over and Happy licks my face.

26
CHAPTER

I must have been out longer than I thought, because when I come back, Mom and the old man are sitting by the kitchen table and eating chicken vegetable soup. She must have been home in between because the old man never has vegetables in his house, only potatoes and meat. Or maybe someone just dropped the soup off. It smells good but I'm not hungry. I stand by the door. The old man and Mom look at me, but neither one says a word. I want to sit with them, make them feel better. But I also want to go home. Alone.

"It was a raven," I finally say.

Mom raises her eyebrows.

"The dogs, they chased a raven, that's why they ran away."

The old man nods.

"He loved the bush," Mom says. "He wouldn't have been happy any other way. He always took you, made you little bows and arrows and slingshots to play with. He called you 'My Little Hunter.' He …"

But I don't want to hear anymore. Not yet.

"I'll see you later at home, okay?" I say and give her a quick hug.

"See you tomorrow, *moshōm*," I say and it sounds good, real. Not like the *moshōms* at school that are only there for a day or two to teach us something. My grandfather will be there whenever I need him. For me and for my mom. I know we will have lots of talks, and I'm kind of looking forward to it, although it's probably going to hurt, too.

But it can wait. All I can think of is to crawl under my blankets and sleep.

CHAPTER 27

The rhythmic tap, tap, tap of the dogs' feet lulls me to sleep. Each time I nod off, the puppy whines and licks my face. Each time, it's harder to wake up. I am so tired. I push the puppy away and free myself of my blankets. The only thing I want now is sleep. The puppy is barking in my ear and turning circles on my chest. I hear a door squeak. Warm strong hands pull me out of the sled. My moshōm*'s hands.*

Suddenly it's warm, so warm my hands and feet hurt. I cry until the pain goes away and then I finally fall asleep. I'm safe now.

★

Barking wakes me up and, for a second, I don't know where I am. But then I see the shelves with my old action figure collection and I know I'm in my bedroom. The door opens and Acimosis runs to my bed to greet me.

"Hey, boy!" I rough him up the way he likes it, kind of like tickling a small child. Then I look up. My mom is standing in the bedroom door. She smiles when she sees my questioning look.

"You always begged me to take him home, but I didn't want a puppy in the house. Now that he isn't a puppy anymore, I thought ..."

I'm out of bed in no time and fling my arms around her.

"Thank you! Thank you!" And then I hesitate. "Can Lightning and Happy and ..."

"Don't even dare to finish that question!" Mom says and tickles me. We both laugh, and Acimosis jumps up on Mom and licks her face. And she doesn't even mind.

ACKNOWLEDGEMENTS

I am greatly indebted to the many northerners who shared their stories about dogs and trapline life with me, thus bringing to life an era that is not as forgotten as it seems.

Tiniki to all the people who shared their stories with me at the finish line of a dog sled race, at a cultural camp, in their homes, on the bus to P.A., in my classroom, during visits to their communities, and on the trails in between. I won't name any people here, simply because the list would be too long. I am always overwhelmed by the northern hospitality and willingness to share homes, food, and stories.

On my quest to find historic records about northern life in

the past, I would like to acknowledge Saskatchewan's publicly accessible archives, especially the "Our Legacy" collection, the "Northern Saskatchewan Archives" and the "Virtual Museum for Métis History and Culture," for all their hard work to catch such an important part of our history before it slips out of our hands.

The paintings Jeremy refers to are by the late Bern Will Brown, who captured his experience of northern life in his art and writing.

On my journey to become a writer, I thank the Canada Council for the Arts for supporting me financially, which gave me the opportunity to seek professional advice at a critical stage of the manuscript.

Thank you to Kathy Stinson and Peter Carver and the participants in the Summer Seaside Writing Retreat for helping me grow as a writer and for believing in me.

Thank you to Lois Dalby, Caron Dubnick, Linda Mikolayenko, Sean Cassidy, Keith Olsen, and Colleen Taylor, for feedback and encouragement.

A special thanks goes to my mentor and editor Peter Carver, who never told me what to do, but always asked me the right questions at the right time. Thank you for helping me to find my voice.

The ones I have to thank most are the ones who will never read this novel: Roscoe, Pompey, Africa, Frank, Cowgirl, Ginger, Happy, Cedric, Piranha, Vicious, Salty, Pepper, Bear, Tobi, Snoopy, Fuzzy, Silu, Lucy, Kakavee, Cheerio, Bizzley, Bandit, Earl, Grace, Mercedes, Gustav, and all the dogs who joined our team on our countless adventures. You are the best trail companions imaginable (you, too, Quincy).

Without you, *Yellow Dog* would never have been written.

MIRIAM KÖRNER

Photo credit: Hannah Taylor

MIRIAM KÖRNER

INTERVIEW WITH MIRIAM KÖRNER

How did you come to know so much about the traditions and culture of the north, including the use of sled dogs?

Foremost by simply living here.

My husband Quincy Miller and I spend a lot of time in the bush, cutting firewood, picking berries and mushrooms, calling moose, setting nets. Quincy grew up in Northern Saskatchewan and he shares his rich cultural heritage with me. We have our own dogs and, in winter, we travel by dog team along the old trails used by generations and generations of First Nations families, trappers, and traders. It's not common to see a dog team in the bush anymore, and lots of time people will stop their skidoos to talk to us—especially the older ones.

"Fine looking dog team you got," someone will say. "I used to have dogs, you know."

And then a story will start. A story that can't be found in history books. The stories bring new life to the fallen-down trapline cabins; they let me see the old trails with new eyes, and they instil in me a deep respect for the working dog teams.

When I realized what a gift those stories were, I made more of an attempt to seek out Elders and find answers to the day-to-day life questions the history books could not answer.

I guess what I know comes from a mix of living a northern lifestyle and listening to stories (which is also part of a northern lifestyle). If I couldn't get a clear enough picture in my head, I would seek out archives and look at old photographs.

I'm still learning.

MIRIAM KÖRNER

Fuzzy relaxing
in the dog yard

What made you want to tell this story?

One winter, I met an Elder in Black Lake who still set his nets

by dog team—using a traditional toboggan, with the dogs

hooked up single file and wearing leather harnesses with

pompoms. I felt as if I had stepped back in time. Here was one

of my heroes of the olden days and he still lived that way. He

was the last one who had a traditional working dog team.

When he died in 2011, I realized what a treasure I had

in all those stories, and I felt it was not mine to keep. At the same time, I wanted to share my own experience of listening to the stories. Last but not least, I wanted to share some of my experiences of working with children exposed to violence, and our sled dogs and the redemptive power the dogs had for those children.

The only way I could see doing that was to do come up with a fictional plot that encompasses all three motives. In a way, it's a natural fit because, up here, people learn through story. The stories are the old man's way of passing his knowledge on to Jeremy and my way of sharing a lifestyle with my readers that very few are fortunate enough to experience.

How common are sled dogs today in the Canadian north?
It's not that long ago that sled dogs were the common mode of winter transportation in the north. Nearly every family had a team, sometimes even two. With the advent of the snowmobile in the 1970s, dog teams quickly disappeared.

Photo credit: Miriam Körner

Gustav and Cheerio enjoying a break on the trail

Today, I don't know of anybody who relies on dogs for hunting or fishing here in Saskatchewan. There are lots of sprint-racing kennels in the northern communities, but even those are becoming less common. Sled dogs are a lot of work and expensive to keep. I know a few mushers who fish for their dogs, but most rely on commercial dog food now.

For the past twelve years, our own dogs earned their own keep by taking tourists out on wilderness adventures, but even businesses like ours are few and far between in Saskatchewan.

It's different in the Yukon and NWT. They have more tourism operations there and big racing kennels that train for mid- and long-distance races like the Iditarod or Yukon Quest.

If you are looking for people who still use dogs traditionally, you would have to go to the Arctic. When I was racing in the Hudson Bay Quest between Churchill, Manitoba, and Arviat, Nunavut, I found the dog culture to be alive and well along the coast of Hudson Bay. I listened to many stories about trapping foxes and hunting polar bears by dog team.

Puppies befriending stray dogs on the street

Photo credit: Miriam Körner

You mention "dog-shooting days." Why does this practice occur?

The first time I heard about dog-shooting days was on the local radio. People were given warning to tie up their dogs or keep them indoors during the three-day shooting. It doesn't take many strays to produce a lot of puppies in a short time. Eight months later, the puppies have puppies and so on. Dogs roam, pack up, and become a danger to children.

I have no doubt that culling will eventually become a thing of the past. More and more communities find alternative ways of dog control, and mobile vet clinics are being offered now in many communities on a regular basis.

Visiting a friend at his remote trapline cabin

What this story is about, above all, is the growth of Jeremy. What is the strongest influence behind his achievement?

Whether he is aware of it or not, Jeremy is on a quest to find himself. He grows from a child that takes things for granted into a young adult that makes conscious choices.

It's impossible to single out the strongest influence. Growth is something that comes from deep within. To me, the experience he has with his dogs and the time he spends with Jack help him to make a connection to his natural environment and to his roots, which are both becoming increasingly important to him. As Jeremy gets to know himself better, his self-esteem grows. He is able to respect himself—and Justin—with all the differences between them.

Why was it important for you to spend time on Justin?

Justin's story is a story, sadly, too many children can relate to. Either they come from a troubled home themselves or know someone who does. As in Justin's case, we don't know their entire story, but we sense that something is not right at home.

It's difficult to break out of the circle of violence, but Justin does. In the end, it's the dogs' gift of unconditional love that redeems Justin. In a way, Justin's growth is even more remarkable than Jeremy's. Jeremy shows us how we can be a reassuring presence in someone's life, while Justin shows us not to let negative experiences take control of our lives.

In many communities, young people don't spend a great deal of time listening to their Elders. What does Jeremy gain from spending time with Jack—the old man who turns out to be his grandfather?

There is a power that comes from personal story, and that power is strongest when it is shared through storytelling. Although

Cold and windy day on Lac La Ronge

Jeremy learns about traditional knowledge in school, he does not connect with it in the same way as he does when the old man passes his skills on to him. It's the context that matters, and Jeremy learns the skills where he will use them—in the bush or on the lake, not in the institution of school.

MIRIAM KÖRNER

Spending time with Jack is not only about learning traditional skills. There is a whole worldview that informs what Jack believes, the way he tells stories, or how he relates to others. The most important lesson that Jeremy learns is about respect. Respecting yourself, other people, animals, and the land. The old man passed on a seed to Jeremy. Now it's up to Jeremy to nurture it and let it grow.

You were not born in Canada, but you have come to adopt this country as your own, a place that gives you a strong sense of belonging. What appeals to you most strongly in the Canadian north?

When I came to Canada, I had no intention of staying here, until I found myself on Bigstone Lake on the coldest and most unforgiving day I have ever experienced.

I was training a team of young dogs for a musher with a big racing kennel. We went north to La Ronge to compete in the Neckbone Sled Dog Race. It was minus-forty degrees when

I was hooking up the dogs. I had frostbite on my nose before I even left the last houses on Fairchild Reserve behind.

The trail led to Bigstone Lake—the ice was windswept and black; the wind was blowing so strong that my sled blew sideways, and there was no trail to tell my dogs where to go. Suddenly, I had this overwhelming feeling that, for the first time in my life, I was where I truly belonged. I've never left.

I think back then I already had a sense that the Canadian north is full of fascinating stories carved onto the land since the beginning of time. What appeals to me most strongly is the widespread understanding that our relationship to the land is reciprocal and, slowly but surely, I leave my own stories scattered across the places I have come to appreciate.

You frequently give presentations to groups of young people. What kind of encouragement do you give those who want to find and tell their own stories?

Quite often when I write, I don't look for stories; the stories

Happy (front centre) and the gang on summer vacation

Photo credit: Miriam Körner

find me. And when that happens, you have to be open to it. Don't think of what other people might think about you or your story. Don't worry about grammar or punctuation. Just let it come out onto the page. Most importantly: Take the time to listen. Sometimes it's yourself you have to listen to, and that's the hardest.

Thank you, Miriam, for your generous insights into life in the North.

Praise for Yellow Dog

*"I found reading Yellow Dog both interesting and nostalgic.
A wonderful tale of maturing, understanding and forgiveness
by renewing a way of life that has all but disappeared ..."*

– Keith Olsen, author of *Within the Stillness: One Family's Winter
on a Northern Trapline*